THE SINGLE WIFE

THE SINGLE WIFE

MARQUITA B.

Corks and Coils Publishing

The Single Wife © 2019 Marquita B.

Published by Corks and Coils Publishing
~ www.corksandcoilspublishing.com

ISBN: (Ebook) 978-1-7330183-0-2

ISBN: (Paperback) 978-1-7330183-1-9

ISBN: (Hardcover) 978-1-7330183-2-6

This is a work of fiction. Any references or similarities to actual events, real people, living or dead or to real locales are used to give a sense of reality. Any similarity in other names, characters, places and incidents is entirely coincidental.

If you purchased this book without a cover, you should be aware that this book is stolen property. It is reported as "unsold" and "destroyed" to the publisher, and neither the author nor the publisher has received payment for this "stripped" book.

Library of Congress Control Number: 2019912828
First printing edition 2019

Dedicated to one of the strongest and most determined people I know, ME
And
To my husband and daughter without which, this book would have been completed much sooner.........
I Love You Both!

INTRODUCTION

I've always dreamed of being a wife. Growing up, the idea of living the single life never once crossed my mind. Being married was always my goal, and to some extent it still is. Maybe it was the fact that I grew up in a home with two parents who, thirty-five years later, remain deeply in love with each other. It may have been something about the way my mother looked at my father when he walked into a room, or the way my father cared for my mother that made me want that for my own life. I guess there's something about the idea of settling down with a "Black Prince Charming" of my own that entices me.

With that said, don't get it twisted. I'm very independent, and I don't need a man in my life for anything. I've always worked hard to ensure that I can provide for myself. Still, the idea of fully submitting to a man turns me on. I enjoy the idea of being pampered and loved on exclusively.

That is what attracted me to Jerell.

In the beginning, Jerell was everything I wanted in a husband, and I looked forward to the day he would propose to me. But that day never came. While he was busy building a foundation for our future instead of putting a ring on it, I watched precious moments slip away. So, after a few years of playing the dating game with no sign of a ring, a void began to form between us. I got tired of being a *girlfriend*, knowing I was wife material. While I still loved Jerell, our relationship no longer excited me. I began to feel as though we kept waiting for the perfect time to marry when we could have already been building our lives together as husband and wife. So, when a new opportunity presented itself, I couldn't help but test the waters.

In retrospect, I feel bad for not ending things with Jerell properly before moving on to someone new. I don't know if it was the "D" or that instant animal-like attraction that I felt for him on sight, but the first time I laid eyes on Kyle, I knew he'd be mine. Unfortunately, in my rush to be a married woman, I ignored every warning sign placed in front of me, and by the time I did see things clearly, I was in way too deep.

They say hindsight is twenty-twenty and, three years later, I can see in my haste to be married that I ended up being nothing more than a single wife. This is my story.

CHAPTER 1

EARLY 2000'S

Before I opened my eyes, I could feel the warmth of the sun's rays beaming upon my face. I'd only slept for about two hours thanks to passionate love-making that lasted until daybreak. Jerell's light breaths danced upon the back of my neck as he slept peacefully beside me. Being together on weekends had become our regular routine since I lived in D.C. and he lived in Virginia.

We'd been together for two years, and while to most people our relationship would be considered perfect, I was beginning to feel as though we'd reached an impasse. It wasn't really anything Jerell had done wrong. He was intellectual, attractive, attentive, and an overall good man. However, I was beginning to have trouble seeing a future with him. He just wasn't moving fast enough for me.

I'd been told a time or two, that I suffered from the Disney syndrome because, ever since I was a little girl, I wanted it all. The perfect husband and the beautiful house in the suburbs, full of kids to love on. I knew the kind of guy I wanted at an early age. I wanted him to be strong, independent, confident, and a provider, like my father. Oh, and he of course needed to be good looking and have some swag. I guess I never considered how hard it would be to get all these characteristics in one man.

My first real relationship was with Stephen. We met after I finished high school. He flirted with me on the regular before I decided to give him the time of day. I was not instantly attracted to him, but his sense of humor and personality eventually won me over. He was a few years older than me and already had a bachelor's degree in Business and a good job. He was educated and made me secure in the fact that he was more than capable of taking care of me. He was an all-around good guy. I told him I loved him but as I look back now, I'm not sure that I did.

However, when Stephen proposed to me, I still said "yes." I guess it was for the sake of security that he gave me. But Stephen had one major flaw. He was a mama's boy, and our entire relationship felt like tug of war between me, him, and his mother. I eventually concluded that Stephen was not the one and I called the wedding off.

Shortly after that, I graduated from Virginia Commonwealth University with a B.S. in Criminal Justice. I moved to

D.C. once I was accepted into Howard's Juris Doctorate program. My goal was to become an attorney. One year into my studies, I accepted a part-time internship with the Attorney General's office. I worked hard, and played hard, spending my weekends hanging out. I'm not going to lie, I was a bit wild during that period, but that ended when I met Jerell.

Jerell was a freelance model I met one Saturday night at Zanzibar. He was five-eleven, with a slim but muscular build. He had the most beautiful and flawless pecan complexion. He sported a low-cut Caesar fade with three-sixty waves, hazel eyes, full lips, and a six pack. I quickly fell head over heels for him. He was ten years older than me, more experienced, and old-school in the way that he treated me. He opened doors for me, had intellectual conversations with me, waited patiently until I was ready to give myself to him sexually, and made me feel safe, secure, and beautiful. He was the epitome of a gentleman. I liked that about him because for a long time I had trouble meeting men who wanted to know me for me and not just for my looks and my figure.

So, when I happened to find a handsome model who was family-oriented, managed his money well, and wanted to know me on a deeper level, I leapt at the opportunity to get to know him better.

During the two years we had been dating, I noticed that Jerell was very strategic. He liked to do everything the right way and he wasn't one for spur-of-the-moment decisions. He liked to take his time, with everything. While in the beginning, I appreciated the fact that he took his time with me, after a while, it began to feel like he was taking too much time, and I just wasn't down to wait.

Even though I was educated and very independent, starting a family was all I really wanted. I knew Jerell wanted the same things I wanted, but Jerell was a planner. He treated life like a game of chess, always waiting to be in the perfect position to make the perfect move. I didn't see life as a strategy like him, though. While he was waiting to make enough money and to be in the ideal place to take care of a wife and kids, I was ready to dive in and experience it all. Why wait when we could build while we were married?

As I continued to think about our relationship, I began to feel more and more discontent. I knew what I wanted, and I knew how to get it, and the more he waited for the right time, the more distance grew between us. I was tired of playing the chess game.

"You up baby?" Jerell's deep voice asked softly into my ear.

"Mhmm," I mumbled.

I could feel his soft kisses on the back of my neck, as tingles traveled down my spine. With all of our issues spiraling in my head, I did not want to cave in, but his lips were insatiable, and I began to get lost in the moment. This was one of the things I loved most about him. His passion for me. He made me forget my thoughts from only moments prior as I got lost in his kisses. I could feel him hardening against the small of my back, and at that moment I decided everything else could wait as he gently placed me on my knees and slid inside of me from behind.

I closed my eyes as a soft moan escaped my lips. *Did I really want to give this man up?* As his strokes increased in pace, I began to get lost in the rhythm of our bodies as we moaned and groaned, meshing into each other until we were a tangled knot of one.

That was the feeling I wanted all the time. I wanted this man to be one with me, in unity and ordained under God as his wife. I no longer wanted to be just a girlfriend.

My core began to pulse intensely, and I could feel myself on the verge of an explosion as my love for him, and my desire for us, overwhelmed me deep into my being.

And even though everything felt right, as we orgasmed together, it all became crystal clear. I could no longer give myself to someone so deeply, without any promise of a future. I needed a ring.

Jerell sat across from me happily eating his breakfast, glancing between his plate and the television, totally oblivious to anything I was thinking. Great sex and all, I needed to let him know that our situation required more forward motion.

He looked up at me and smiled as he caught my gaze. "What's up, Kia? Something on your mind?"

Now or never. Tell him what you want, girl.

"Uh, yeah. Actually, there is. Jerell, I love you—."

"I know. And I love you too, Kia," he interrupted, his demeanor changing when he added, "But I know that's not what you want to say."

"Yeah, it's not. There's more. Like I was saying, I love you, but I want more. You're a great man, but we've been together for two years now, and I have no clue what our future together holds. I guess I just need some confirmation as to what your plans are for our future. I just want to make sure we're on the same page."

Jerell put his fork down and stared into his plate for a moment before speaking. "Kia, you are the woman I want to build a life with. I know you might think now is as good a time as any to get married, but we haven't even set a solid foundation for us to build from yet. Every move I make is to get myself closer to the goal of being financially ready to make you my wife. It may seem like we're wasting time, but believe me, we have our entire lives ahead of us—together. I know what kind of upbringing you had, and I want to give you the world the same way your father gave your mother the world. It would be irresponsible of me to marry you now. I really want to marry you, I'm simply not financially ready I have nothing to offer you yet."

"Jerell, all I need is you. Our love is a solid enough foundation. We can build together by working and saving money. We are all we need," I pleaded with him. *Didn't he know that our love was all we needed? Didn't he know that I'd hold him down just like I knew he'd hold me down and that us working together was enough?*

"Let's be real, Nakia. Love isn't going to pay the bills. You're working on your master's. We're still working toward our goals. I know you want it all now, but I promise you, I'm not going anywhere. Trust me when I tell you, it's better to take our time and make sure everything is in place before we make such a big move that we might regret later."

It was at that moment that Jerell saw the look on my face and realized he'd made a mistake.

"A move we might regret?" I could not believe the words coming from his mouth. "Oh, okay. I got it. So, basically, you're not really sure if you want to marry me?"

Jerell lowered his head. "I didn't mean it like that, Kia. I simply meant we should make sure we are more established before we make such an important move. I don't want to set us up for failure. I watched my parents' marriage get torn apart as they stressed over bills and trying to make ends meet. I don't want that type of life for us. I want us to be secure and ready to take on the world when we get married. I just don't think now is the time."

I thought for a moment before rising, without a word, from the table.

"C'mon. Don't be like that. Sit back down and let's finish talking this out."

"It's okay. I understand. There really isn't much more to say, is there?" I grabbed my plate and headed to the kitchen.

I finally knew the truth. Even though Jerell wanted the same things I wanted, we weren't in sync in how to when to get there, and his idea of happiness was far different from mine. Tomorrow wasn't promised, and I wasn't about to let any more time slip away from me. I was going to have everything I wanted even if it wasn't with Jerell.

CHAPTER 2

Jerell must have sensed my discontent because he headed back home to Virginia earlier than planned. I cleaned up the mess from breakfast before pouring a glass of wine and turning on sweltering hot water for a bubble bath. As the water ran, I gazed at myself in the mirror. I had gained 10 pounds, in all the right spots, since meeting Jerell and the curvy coke bottle physique and coco completion I flaunted still looked damn good. We spent so much time boo'd-up in our apartments that the club scene became a thing of the past. I hated the gym but loved to dance so the club was always a full workout for me. I dropped it like it was hot on the regular and the looks of my behind and waist to hip ratio could vouch for that.

The steam from the bath had the mirror slightly fogged as I got in. The water was scalding hot just the way I liked it. Taking a bath was my escape. A chance to clear my mind if only for a few moments. I sipped my wine, soaked and meditated.

As the water became cool, I slowly came back to reality, let out the water and took a shower. As I got dressed, I thought about Jerell. I poured another glass of wine before retreating to the sofa. I needed to figure out how to end things with Jerell and before I could ponder a thought, my phone rang.

"Hey, girl. What you up to?" my friend Toni asked.

"Hey, friend. Nothing much just sipping some wine.

"Of course, you are doing your favorite pastime."

"SIPPING WINE," we both shouted in unison.

"Bo-ring," Toni teased through the phone. "But anyway girl, I was calling to see if you want to ride down to Myrtle Beach with me and a few friends next weekend?"

"Girl, you're driving all the way to Myrtle Beach and back for basically two days? Nah, I'm cool. You are doing a lot for someone that has to go to work on Monday morning."

"Uh, you know I am talking about Memorial Day weekend, right? That means no work on Monday; a three-day weekend. Girl, where you been?"

"Oh, damn." With everything going on with Jerell, I had forgotten all about the upcoming long weekend. "You're right. I totally forgot next Monday is a holiday."

"Yes girl! So, are you coming or what? I haven't seen your ass in a minute, and you need a break from being cooped up in that little apartment of yours with Jerell every weekend."

"Who you telling? Hmmm?" I knew there was nothing but

temptation at the beach, but I really needed a breather from Jerell. "Yeah I guess I'll go. But you coming to get me, right? I'm not trying to drive all the way down to Myrtle Beach and back by myself."

"Yeah, yeah. I'll pick you up. I'm actually renting a van, and we're all driving down together."

"Who is *all* Toni?" I began to wonder if going away with Toni and her friends for the weekend was a good idea. I'd met some of Toni's friends in the past and, while I'm always down for a good time, some of them were a bit too extra for my taste. I also hated drama and if Toni was heading to the beach with girls who loved drama, I wasn't interested.

"Oh, just a few friends, and friends of friends. I promise you; everyone is cool. We're just a bunch of young professionals looking to have a nice, relaxing weekend. Nothing more."

I had a feeling Toni was making that face she made when she was up to something, but I agreed anyway.

"Okay, girl. So when should I be ready? I can leave work early on Friday if necessary."

"Good, because I'll be there to get you around two."

"Cool, I'll leave work at noon. I can't wait to see you, get some sun on the beach, and just relax! This internship and this situation with Jerell have been stressing me the hell out."

"Wait—situation with Jerell? What happened? Do I need to come kick somebody's ass?"

"No, no. It's not like that. Look, I don't want to get into it right now. I'll catch you up on everything this weekend."

"Oh okay, girl, just checking, because you know I fight men, right?"

We both laughed. I'd only known Toni since undergrad, but she was definitely a true friend. We'd shared a lot of fun times together and gotten into some crazy shit too, so I was excited to be able to see her because I knew I was in for a good time.

After chatting with Toni for a little while longer, we hung up, and I threw some clothes in the wash. Then I called my parents, made a quick salad for dinner, and prepared myself mentally for the long week ahead.

As I laid down in my bed, I could smell Jerell's scent on the pillow. Tears welled up in my eyes as I thought about life without him. I would miss his chivalry, the way he made me feel and our intellectual conversations. *Was I ready to let this man go?* After making up my mind that I would wait until I returned from my trip to end things with Jerell, I clicked off my TV and fell asleep.

Not more than a half hour later, I was awakened by my phone ringing. I reached for the phone on my nightstand and looked at the caller ID. It was Jerell, and I didn't want to talk to him. I placed the cordless phone back down on the receiver and waited for my answering machine to pick up.

"Hey, it's Nakia. I can't answer your call, but please leave a message, and I'll get back to you as soon as I can. Talk to you soon."

"Hey, it's me. I guess you're already asleep. Look, I hate how

our conversation ended earlier. Nakia, I promise you're the only woman I love and the only woman I want to marry. When I said I didn't want us to have regrets, I meant I didn't want you to regret marrying me if I wasn't able to provide for you the way I know I should—the way I want to. I hope you understand and know that we will get married. I think we just need a little bit more time. Please be patient with me for a little while longer. Okay, I'll talk to you tomorrow. Call me when you get home from work... I love you, baby."

I couldn't help but feel sad as I listened to Jerell's message. My feelings were already changing for him. Just as fast as I'd fallen in love with him two years prior, I was falling out of love with him. I just couldn't be with a man that wasn't willing to commit to me fully. There were plenty of fish in the ocean and I'd learned how to fish for what I wanted at an early age. While I was disappointed that I wouldn't be Jerell's wife, I was beginning to feel optimistic about what was to come. Still, I was a little bit conflicted about whether or not I was making a mistake. To calm my nerves, I decided to pray.

"Dear God, please guide my path and help me to make the right decisions. If I'm supposed to be with Jerell, please give me a sign. And if Jerell isn't the one for me, please send me my Black Prince Charming. May he be my Boaz and not a bozo. All I want is a man who is willing to commit and put a ring on it. Thank you for hearing my prayer. Amen."

CHAPTER 3

The week went by faster than I expected. I was so busy reviewing case files and reviewing witness testimonies, that by the time I left for the day, I only had time to eat, take a shower, and go to bed. The attorney I interned for had a heavy case load, so I worked late most of the week. I was so busy that I didn't even make time to talk to Jerell, but as Thursday night rolled around, I knew I needed to call him to at least let him know I'd be gone for the weekend. To be honest, I was surprised he hadn't popped up at my apartment after I'd ignored him all week. He had not called me again since leaving the voicemail message. So, I picked up the phone, took a deep breath, and dialed his number. He picked up after the first ring.

"So, you finally decided to call me back?"

There was something in his tone that said he knew things

weren't quite right between us and possibly never would be again. It was as if he was defeated.

"Hey," I said, ignoring the accusation. *What did he want me to do? Apologize? He's the one that didn't know what he wanted, not me.* "I just wanted to let you know that I'm leaving town for a few days tomorrow."

"Oh, yeah?"

"Yeah. My girl Toni called last Sunday and invited me on a trip down to Myrtle Beach for the weekend. I'm just going to go and relax for a while. I need some time to think and get my mind right."

There was an uncomfortable pause before he finally spoke "Why does it feel like you want to break up with me?"

I don't know, maybe because I do? "Look, I just need some time to think. That's all. I'll call you when I get back." I didn't want to be rude, but I also didn't want to have that conversation with him right then. He was a good guy and had always been good to me, but I needed time to think. Patience isn't one of my virtues and I figured the time away would allow me to reflect.

"Okay, have fun," Jerell said with annoyance. "I guess I'll talk to you when you get back."

"Okay, I will call you."

"Oh, and Nakia?"

"Yeah?"

"Don't do anything I wouldn't do..."

There was a pause as I considered my response. The nerve of him! What he wouldn't do is commit.

"Look, I'll call you when I get back. I'm tired so I'm about to get ready for bed. I just wanted to call you to let you know about my plans."

"Wait, Nakia?"

"Yes, Jerell?"

"I love you. You know, that right?"

I took a deep breath and I tried to hold in my tears. "Yeah, I know. I'll talk to you soon," I replied quickly before the tears came. I had barely clicked "end" on the phone before my face was flooded. As much as I loved Jerell, I knew I couldn't be with him anymore. I'd made up my mind that as soon as I returned from the beach, I'd break up with him. I just wanted to do it in person and not on the phone. He deserved that much.

Friday morning flew by just as fast as the earlier part of the week had, and before I knew it, I was at home packing-up a few last-minute things before Toni arrived. It was barely two when I heard banging on my apartment door.

"C'mon girl. Open this door! I gotta pee," Toni yelled from the other side of the door.

I opened the door, and she flew past me to the bathroom.

"Well, hello to you too," I laughed.

A few moments later, she reemerged and gave me a hug.

"Hey, girl. My bad. I been holding it for like an hour. You ready?"

"Sure am."

After making sure I had everything, I locked up, and Toni and I headed down. As soon as we reached the van, I couldn't help but shake my head. The van was packed.

"Who are these people?" I asked after elbowing Toni.

She said nothing verbally but gave me a mischievous smirk before boarding.

As I entered the van and maneuvered my way to the only empty seat in the back row, I caught a glimpse of the sexiest man I'd seen in a while in the seat right next to the one I'd be sitting in. My heartbeat pounded as I took in how gorgeous he was. Even while sitting down, I could tell he was tall. His frame was strong and thick, and I was hypnotized by the muscles protruding from beneath his wife-beater. His skin was a deep mahogany tone, and he had intense dark brown almond-shaped eyes, luscious full lips and a nicely trimmed full beard and mustache. He was a grown ass man, and I bit my lip as I imagined all the grown-up things we could do to together.

I must have been staring because he caught my gaze and smiled. Pristinely white teeth only added to the perfection of the man he was.

"Is this enough room for you?" he asked as he eyed me up and down before licking those luscious lips of his.

I wanted to feel them pressed against mine and everywhere else on my body.

"Yes, that's fine," I replied as I regained my composure and sat down next to him. I just knew he could hear how fast my heart was beating in my chest. I hadn't been that excited by a man since the day I met Jerell.

Oblivious to my heated attraction, Toni began to introduce us all. I learned the fine-ass man beside me was named Kyle, and he was a friend-of-a-friend of Toni's. As we began to drive toward the beach, I tried my best to play it cool, but in the back of my mind I couldn't help but think of the possibilities. Something about the way he looked at me let me know I had piqued his interest just as much as he'd piqued mine.

"So, are you from D.C.?" Kyle asked, interrupting my thoughts.

"Oh, ummm, my family is in Richmond. I moved here to go to Howard. What about you?"

"Yeah, I'm from Richmond too. But I'll be honest, you don't sound like you're from Richmond, and I know everyone worth knowing in Virginia, so there's no way you're from Richmond because I'd know you."

I couldn't help but smile. "Yeah well my family moved to Richmond from Jersey when I was a teenager."

Ever since I'd moved to Richmond, people had always talked about my accent. While it wasn't as strong as it used to be, it was still noticeable.

"Oh, okay. So, you're a Jersey girl?" he replied, blinding me with those radiant teeth.

"Yeah, is that a problem?" I asked with a crooked eyebrow.

"Nah, it's definitely not a problem. Jersey makes some fine women, I see."

If my chocolate skin could blush, I'm sure it would've been. This man was obviously flirting with me, and I was loving every minute of it.

As everyone else chatted away, Kyle and I engaged in small talk. I learned that he was single with no kids and that he shared a "bachelor pad," as he put it, with his father who he'd recently reconnected with. He was raised by a single mom and didn't really deal with his father until he was an adult. He worked as a supervisor in a call center and only knew Toni through one of his good friends.

I told him a little bit about myself and my family. I left out the part about having a boyfriend though. As far as I was concerned, my status was about to change to single anyway. Besides, it was only a weekend. No harm in keeping a few things to myself. It's not like I would ever see him again anyway.

At some point during the ride, I must have nodded off because I woke up just as we arrived at the hotel, and of course, I just happened to have been resting my head on Kyle's chest.

"My bad. I didn't mean to be laying all on you. To be honest, I don't even remember falling asleep."

"It's all good, shorty. You look cute when you sleep," Kyle replied, flashing that beautiful smile of his again.

All I could do was smile back and gaze in awe at how fine he was.

"Okay, guys. Let's get it!" Toni yelled excitedly from the front of the van. "After everyone's checked into their rooms, let's meet downstairs in the lounge around ten for dinner and drinks. I hear the lounge turns into a club after eleven, so I'll see you guys in a little bit."

I glanced at my watch. It was a little after nine, leaving me with only a little bit of time to freshen up. I hadn't been out in a while and wanted to get dressed in something sexy. After all I knew Kyle would be watching and there was something about him that turned me on. A little innocent flirting would help me clear my mind of Jerell.

After taking a quick shower and throwing on a sexy black mini dress that accentuated my curves, some open-toed high heels, and a dab of makeup, I did a quick check in the mirror before heading downstairs to the lobby to meet everyone in the lounge. On my way to the elevator, I ran into Toni, on her way down as well.

"Hey, girl. Look at you, looking all good and shit," Toni teased as we entered the elevator and hit the button for the lobby.

"We did not have much time, so I just threw something on real quick. You look good as well."

"Uh-uh heffa, don't act like you didn't dress up for no reason. I caught you casually falling asleep on Kyle's chest. What's all that about? If I'm not mistaken, don't you have a man, Miss. Thang?"

The reminder of resting on Kyle's hardened muscles sent

heat through my body, but because of Toni's accusatory tone, I felt like I needed to defend myself. "I did not fall asleep on that man's chest on purpose. It was definitely an accident."

"Yeah, yeah. Accident my ass. Anyway, you never told me. What's up with you and Jerell?"

"Girl, it's a lot. But, to make a long story short, I'm just tired of waiting around for him to make the next move. If I left it up to him, we'd be dating until we're forty and I don't have time for that. Honestly, I'm planning on breaking up with him when I get home. I love him, but I don't think we're on the same page anymore as far as our futures are concerned."

"I'm sorry to hear that Kia. I always thought you two would grow old together. I understand though. But, to be honest, you really shouldn't be trying to settle down with anyone, anyway."

I couldn't help but wonder if Toni had a point. At only twenty-three, what was I thinking about settling down and getting married for? I had my whole life ahead of me. Maybe I was tripping and Jerell was right. *Was I moving too fast? Would breaking up with Jerell be the biggest mistake of my life?*

We exited the elevator and proceeded directly ahead to the lounge. The rest of the group was already waiting for us at a table, but I saw only Kyle. He was dressed in a white dress shirt, unbuttoned at the top and fitted to his muscular frame beautifully. I could see the outline of his chest penetrating the fabric. The splotches on his jeans weren't the distasteful stains of someone careless but rather the faded marking of designer clothing. He topped it off with designer dress shoes. He really cared about how he presented himself and I'm not exaggerating, he was definitely the flyest man in the entire room. His eyes were directly on me and they devoured me as I walked toward the table, like I was a meal he couldn't wait to taste. By the way I was feeling, I'm not sure I would have stopped him if he'd taken a bite right then and there. My mind was clear, and my mood was laxed. I came to the beach to have some innocent fun. I was en route to being single for the first time in two years so thinking about Jerell was not an option. Besides the desire building between Kyle and I was electric, and I was sure everyone else noticed it as well.

Toni sat in a seat next to one of the women in our group, leaving only one seat left. As I walked toward the empty seat beside Kyle, he stood up and pulled it out for me.

"Thank you," I said.

"My pleasure."

I sat down and caught a whiff of his cologne. It was not too strong and definitely not cheap. It was tastefully applied, and it smelled delicious. His scent was so intoxicating, I didn't realize our waitress had arrived to take our drink order until Kyle called my name.

"Nakia? I think she's waiting for your order."

"Oh, I'm sorry. I'll have what she's having," I motioned toward Toni. I had no clue what Toni had ordered, and after the waitress left, I realized I'd made a mistake considering how Toni drank.

"You look amazing by the way," Kyle said softly. Tingles

went up and down my body as his breath grazed across my skin, the scent of mint filling the air every time he spoke.

"Thank you," I replied, bashfully.

As our group talked, drank, ate, and laughed, I lost count of how many drinks I'd ordered. I didn't realize how tipsy I was until Kyle asked me to dance and I stood up. Somehow, I made it to the dance floor where we grinded on each other and even two-stepped for what felt like hours. By the time we sat down to take a break, it was almost closing time, and as I looked around, I realized everyone in our group had already retired to their rooms, including Toni.

"Damn, it looks like we're all alone," Kyle said with a glint of mischief in his eyes.

"I see. I guess I should be heading back to my room as well. I already know I'm going to have the worst hangover in the morning, and I can guarantee you that Toni already has a whole day of activities planned for us."

"Yeah, I'm sure she does. Well, let me walk you back to your room. What floor are you on?"

"I'm in room 1001. What about you?"

"I'm in room 1101, so I'm guessing I'm right on top of you."

We both laughed at the "right on top of you" part.

"Well, not on top of you, but—I mean I—well, you know what I meant."

Okay, that's enough. Time to go. This man is going to get me into trouble.

"Okay, on that note, I think it's really time I head to my

room, sir." I said in an attempt to dial back the all too relaxed nature of the evening. "But you don't have to walk me to my room. I'll be alright. The elevator is fine. You don't have to go out of your way."

I rose from my seat, and stumbled over my own feet, and Kyle put his arm around me to stabilize me.

"Hmm, I think I'd better walk you to your room, just to be on the safe side."

I nodded in agreement.

As we walked toward the elevator, my heart was racing. I had no clue what Kyle was doing to me, but internally I was losing it. My body was on fire and I couldn't tell if it was the liquor, my hormones, or both. I had no idea what I wanted from him, but I did know I enjoyed his company, and the fact that he was easy on the eyes made things even more complicated. However, inviting him into my room was definitely out of the question. *How would it look if I invited a man I'd just met back to my room? What would he think of me?*

We exited the elevator and walked toward my room. On the way, I stopped and took off my heels.

"I give excellent foot massages, just so you know," Kyle said, with a grin. I guess he could tell by the way I was walking that my feet were killing me.

"Hmm," I teased. "I bet you do. Sounds like you're trying to get into my room, mister?"

"I'm gonna be real. I'm trying to get into more than just your room," Kyle replied staring intensely into my eyes. By the time we were standing outside my room, I could feel my stomach doing flips while I imagined Kyle's body against mine.

Before I could respond, Kyle pulled me close and took my bottom lip into his mouth. A jolt of electricity went through my body as I relaxed into his embrace and our tongues danced together in a passionate rhythm I'd never experienced before. My mind told me to stop but my body was begging for more. I could feel his hands grab onto my ass. My stomach flipped as he pulled me even closer. Our bodies pressed tightly together, I felt his bulge harden against me.

A soft moan escaped my lips as I became overwhelmed by the energy between us. This wasn't right. I needed to leave one situation before considering another. I finally convinced myself to pull away.

"Wait, Kyle. I can't."

"What's wrong?" he asked, pulling me back into him.

I gently pushed him away again. "I have to be honest. I kinda have a boyfriend. I shouldn't be doing this. This is wrong."

"It didn't feel wrong to me."

"So, are you saying you don't care that I have a man?"

"I'm saying that any man that allows a woman as fine as you to go on a group trip to the beach without him is crazy as hell. If you were mine, I'd never let you leave my sight."

I didn't have a response. Jerell was such a good man, but the feelings I had just experienced with Kyle were way more intense than they were with Jerell, and I barely knew Kyle. *How was that possible?*

"Don't worry. I'm not trying to break up a happy home. I'll see you tomorrow, Nakia," Kyle said, before kissing me on the forehead and walking back towards the elevator.

I closed the door behind me and in the darkness of my room I let out a deep sigh of relief. But at the same time, it took everything I had in me not to run out into the hallway and call Kyle back. I was so confused.

Damn, this man is something else, I thought before heading to the bathroom to take a cold shower. I had no doubt in my mind that Kyle was doing the same—and maybe a bit more.

CHAPTER 4

Surprisingly, I woke up the next morning around ten feeling refreshed with no hangover. The group had planned on meeting in the lobby for brunch, so after showering, I threw on a black bikini, some denim cutoffs, and flip-flops, grabbed my bag and beach towel, and headed downstairs.

Like last night, I was the last one to arrive, and Kyle was there flashing his trademark smile as he motioned for me to sit next to him. I couldn't help but notice two of the girls in our group giving me judgmental stares. I didn't care, hell they did not know me, and I had no intentions on getting to know them or anyone else in the group this weekend. Kyle seemed oblivious to it all. I ignored the looks and tried to remain calm with the intention of downplaying things with Kyle.

"So, how did you sleep?" he asked, as I sat down next to

him. His tone was slightly awkward, which considering last night was not a surprise.

"Great, and you?"

"It was alright. I was a bit hot though, so I took a cold shower to cool off."

I was grateful that the dark pigments of my skin concealed the heat rising from my face. "Likewise," was all I could reply.

After brunch, we all hopped into the van and headed to the beach. It was a steamy ninety degrees outside, but only the men were thinking about getting in the water. Though I had on my bikini, I had no intentions of getting wet. I simply wanted to look cute, feel the warmth of the sun, and relax on the beach. But the way Kyle was looking at me as I stripped off my cutoffs told me he had other things in mind.

As I sat on top of the beach towel that I'd set in the warm sand, I noticed one of my bikini strings was loose. While adjusting the string, I felt Kyle's presence behind me. Before I could turn around, he had knelt behind me.

"Let me help you with that," he said, placing his hands over mine and tightening my bikini string. The way his hands felt as they graced my neck turned me on. I wished we were alone on the beach, so I could do every little naughty thing I'd been thinking about since the night before, but I tried maintaining my composure.

"So, why are you single?" I blurted out.

"I don't know. I guess I just haven't found someone I want to settle down with...yet."

"Hmm, I see."

"So, now I have a question for *you*. Why are you still in a relationship? It's obvious you're unhappy or he'd be here with you? What did he do?"

I took a drink from my water bottle before I answered. "It's not what he did, it's more like what he didn't do."

"What? Is the sex lame?"

"No, it's not that," I laughed. "It's more like I want to be at a different place in our relationship than where we are. We've been dating for two years, and I just think we should've made more progress. I don't know, maybe I'm just moving too fast."

"Nah, I understand. You want what you want. You're kind of like me. When I know I've met the right woman, I'm immediately asking myself if she is wife material. I'm not interested in playing the dating game. I'm not an indecisive person at all. When I see something—or someone—I want, I do what I have to do to get it."

"Is that right?" I asked jokingly to soften the mode.

"Yes. I'm a very determined man. And right now, I'm curious to see how far I can get with you, Nakia."

I swallowed, hard. Things were progressing farther than I had anticipated this morning. Kyle was saying all of the right things, but his intentions were still unclear to me. It sounded like he wanted to take me from my man, and I did not know how I felt about that.

"I think I'm going to go get my feet wet," I said quickly, before rising and heading toward the shoreline.

As I stood at the edge of the shore, the waves crashing on my toes, I couldn't help but think about Jerell. While I had pretty much made up my mind that things were over between us, I knew it would be wrong to take things to another level with Kyle without properly ending things with Jerell first. But the sexual tension between Kyle and I was rising. He was making it difficult for me to restrain myself. He was saying all the right things. I was on the verge of exploding, and I knew if Kyle continued being Mr. Perfect, we'd wind up exploding together, in one of our beds.

As if on cue, I felt Kyle walk up behind me and pull me back into him. Being wrapped in his arms felt like unexplainable bliss, and even though I barely knew him, I felt so safe when I was in his embrace. I was melting in his arms and my thoughts of Jerell seemed to fade. I knew everyone was probably watching us, including Toni, but at that point, I didn't care who saw. Everything just felt right.

"Damn, it's hot out here," I absently said out loud.

"Well, let's get wet then," Kyle said before suddenly lifting me up and carrying me into the water.

I screamed and snickered excitedly as the cold waves splashed against my skin. Once he was waist-deep, he lowered me down into the water. I shivered, due to the shock of the chilled water wrapped around me. Kyle pulled me in close to his embrace again, but this time we were standing face to face. *Is this really happening? Am I really letting go of —*

Before I could finish my thought, he pulled my face in close and kissed me softly on the lips. He followed up with another kiss that was long and passionate, before nibbling on my bottom lip. His tongue slipped in against mine, as if he were finishing what we started the night before. I didn't know what was happening—not with my relationship with Jerell, not with what the other people in our group were doing or thinking, not even what this meant for Kyle and I, but I relaxed and decided to let it happen.

I realized I wouldn't be sleeping alone that night.

The two of us rode back with the group to the hotel in silence. I half-listened as the others made plans to head over to a nearby club, but I didn't care. Kyle and I had unspoken plans of our own. At first, I felt a little guilty about Jerell, but I was too hot, and nothing was going to stop what was about to go down between me and Kyle. It was like it was all meant to be, at least, that's what I had convinced myself.

Soon after, we arrived back at the hotel, the two of us wasted no time slipping away, and headed to Kyle's room. He had barely closed the door to his suite before we were pulling each other's clothes off. The electricity between us was at an all-time high, and it was only seconds before we were both standing naked in front of each other. As Kyle stood across from me, I took in the part of him I'd never seen before. The part of him I had only felt. Long, thick and ebony. From the looks of things, he was excited to meet me.

The expression on Kyle's face let me know he was happy with what he saw. He looked up and down my naked body and it seemed as if he was deciding where to explore first.

I was surprised by my confidence. Yes, I had a nice body, but like every other woman, I had my insecurities. Growing up as a brown-skinned girl with a beautiful light-skinned mother, it took me a long time to believe that beauty comes in all shades of brown. I also had a big butt and had been teased all throughout my childhood. For a long time, I hadn't been very comfortable in my skin and damn sure wouldn't have stood naked in front of a man as fine as Kyle. I mean, Jerell was handsome as well, but he didn't have the swag that Kyle did, and to me Kyle's charm was the game changer. He made me comfortable. I let down my guard and released my inhibitions with no questions asked. As I watched Kyle gaze in awe at my brown skin and curves, I felt like the sexiest woman in the world.

My breathing increased when Kyle lifted me up and laid me gently on the bed. Then he spread my legs and begin kissing and licking my inner thighs and working his way up. I let out a moan as his tongue dived deep inside of me. I could feel passion spilling out of my core as he quenched his thirst between my legs. His finger strummed on my pearl, as I held onto the back of his head. The slurping noises he made as he drank me up were a turn on. He was feasting and did not waste a drop. My toes clenched as I neared an orgasm, but before I reached my climax, Kyle maneuvered me further back on the bed, and climbed on top of me.

He wrapped his mouth around one of my 36-DD breasts, his fingers continuing where his mouth had left off moments before, he sucked and nibbled on my large nipples making every attempt to wrap his lips around my adequately sized areolas until pleasure burst from my center.

I could no longer contain myself. I opened my legs wider, inviting him inside of me. The invitation was not wasted, and I felt his hardness plunge into me.

I moaned his name like I'd been waiting for him my entire life. His strokes were slow at first, before increasing in pace, and the faster he stroked, the closer I was to my climax. I could feel my juices pouring down my inner thigh as I tried my best to contain the jolts of pleasure thrashing inside of me. Suddenly, we were both there. My body began to fill up with electricity, and a wave of euphoria came over me unlike any I had ever experienced before. He was giving me life.

As we both came down from our high, a surge of energy rushed through me again and I wanted more. I quickly maneuvered myself on top of him and eased him back inside of me. I grinded my hips slowly at first, then I closed my eyes and bit my lip before rocking faster. As I began to get into my groove, he smacked my ass and I began to ride him even harder and faster. Our moans were loud, and I just knew we were going to get a call from the front desk at any moment. I began to feel myself on the verge of another orgasm, and as my body succumbed to the energy tingling inside of me, I collapsed onto his chest as both of us climaxed again.

The next couple of hours were filled with round after round of exploring each other in every angle imaginable until neither one of us could move. Finally, after one of the most powerful orgasms I'd ever had, we fell asleep, the both of us spent from a passion neither one of us could have imagined. It was like our bodies were made for each other, and from that moment on, I had a feeling that our lives would be intertwined.

CHAPTER 5

I have always prided myself in being a good girl. Before my encounter with Kyle, I'd never cheated on any man I'd ever dated. To be honest, other than Jerell, I'd only seriously dated one other person, and that was Stephen.

When I first met Jerell, we had taken things slow. We had been nine months into our relationship before we had sex for the first time, and Jerell never rushed me. I guess that was one of the reasons why I'd fallen for him so hard. He'd respected me and had been willing to wait for me. I appreciated that.

However, Jerell was several years older than me, and sometimes I think he treated me with kid gloves. When I was with Jerell, I felt like a china doll. While sex with him was good, it sometimes felt as if he handled me with too much care. Kyle, on the other hand, sexed me like I was grown. There was an animal-like attraction between us that I felt from the first time I saw him. So, when we were bound together in passion, it was like we were feeding some supernatural energy that only the two of us shared. Destiny would be the best word to explain how perfectly things aligned for Kyle and I, initially. And when I found out we were both Geminis, born only a week apart, it basically sealed our fates.

From that weekend at Myrtle Beach on, Kyle and I were a couple, and Jerell soon became a distant memory.

A few days after I returned from Myrtle Beach, Jerell got his first big break. He was offered a modeling gig overseas. I decided not to break things off with him because I didn't want to ruin his good news. To my relief, he had to leave immediately, so I didn't have to see him face-to-face. He promised to call as much as he could, and he did, but I was wrapped up in work and Kyle, and the time difference didn't help either. I must admit, I didn't return his phone calls, so we ended up not talking at all. It made things easier that way. In my mind, we'd both moved on without having a long, drawn-out discussion.

In the meantime, Kyle and I linked up a few weeks after the beach trip. From there we spent every bit of our free time together and when we weren't together, we stayed on the phone for hours on end. For our first date, I met up with him in Richmond for a romantic dinner at *Bone Fish*. We flirted, laughed, and talked about our past, and what we wanted in the future. After dinner, we grabbed ice cream from a vendor outside of the restaurant, and window-shopped at the attached outdoor *Short Pump* mall.

"I hope you are having a good time, Kia," he said with a serious expression on his face.

"I am having a great time. Getting to know you on a deeper level has been nice. I feel like I have learned more about you in the last month than I did in two years with my ex." You are like an open book and that has caused me to be open."

"I am glad you feel that way because I really see a future with you." We stopped walking and faced each other. "I already know you are the woman for me. You're going to be my wife one day," he said as he grabbed my hand.

I was melting internally and deep down I felt the same way. "I want the same thing," I said, leaning in for a kiss. The kiss lasted for what seemed to be a lifetime.

We headed back to his place, which he shared with his dad. He led me into a home that was clean and nicely laid out with leather furniture, a pool table, and sports knick-knacks. It was a true bachelor's pad. The house was empty, and you could hear a pin drop. We went through the kitchen and up the stairs to a large room with an en suite.

"Wow how did you master getting the master bedroom," I teased.

"My dad had the house built and put two masters in the plan. Do you have any other questions?" He asked licking his lips.

I made a sexy chuckle, letting him know that I knew what time it was. He wrapped his arms around my waist from behind and walked me into the bathroom while kissing my neck. He opened the glass door to the shower and turned on the water.

"Make it hot," I forcefully suggested.

"I got you," he said while unzipping my dress and then kneeling down to remove my shoes.

"No panties, no bra." He said excitedly as I lifted the dress over my head.

"This dress is skin tight and as long as my breast are riding high, I don't need to wear a bra with it and I didn't want to have an underwear line," I explained while hopping into the over-sized shower. "So, when is your dad coming home?"

"He is gone for the weekend. His room is at the other end of the house anyway so it's all good," he said while lathering soap and a washcloth and beginning to wash me.

We cleaned each other while rubbing, touching kissing. When we rinsed off, I was wet, and it was not from the water. The steam from the water continued to rise as he backed me up against wall of the shower and I flinched as it was cold. He kissed me fervently before hoisting me up in the air and placing my legs on his shoulders. He gently French kissed the lips of my yoni before making his way to my pearl. I yelped in pleasure repeatedly while grabbing his arms, which were around my waist for support. I was so hot and bothered that I quickly began to appreciate the cold shower wall against my back. This man was making love to my yoni with his mouth and I lost count of how many times I climaxed. He lowered me down and I could barely stand as my legs were quivering. He placed me on my knees in the floor of the shower he laid down and maneuvered his mouth back to where he had left off. His long tongue penetrated me, and I rode it reverse cowgirl style until I could no longer hold myself up. As I leaned forward to place his manhood into my mouth, he stopped me.

"No, tonight is all about you, my love."

I stood and rinsed off with his help. He wrapped me in a towel as we headed back to the bedroom.

"Lay down," he motioned towards the bed as he put in Musiq SoulChild's latest, *Luvanmusiq*.

"I'm falling in love with you, Kia," he whispered in my ear before gently entering me. He took his time and engaged every part of my body. He said he loved me, and my mind, body and soul could feel it with every intentional stroke. I was falling for him too, and before the end of the night, I let him know it.

CHAPTER 6

I was in bliss; things with Kyle were going great and we were in the midst of the holiday season. It felt good to be with someone with similar ambitions and the same energetic spirit as my own. Kyle was the same age as I was, and that may have been why I related to him a little more than I did Jerell. And the Gemini thing made things even more interesting. It was almost like we were two sides of one whole. Kyle had not yet met anyone from my family or any of my friends—other than Toni—so, when I received a wedding invitation in the mail from my girl Rae, I figured it was a good opportunity to bring him around some friends.

I walked into the small chapel with the most delicious looking arm candy and was immediately approached by Toni. We hugged.

"I see you all are doing well. You two make me sick, all lovey-dovey and such. You better be treating my friend right," she teased.

We all laughed.

"We are in a really good place," I replied before we headed in to be seated.

The wedding was quaint and beautiful, with just close family and friends attending. Kyle and I held each other tightly as the vows were stated. Rae and her soon-to-be husband, Marco, were true life goals.

At the reception, I introduced Kyle to everyone as we ate, drank, and had a great time. Although Kyle was grilled with questions the whole night, he was received well by everyone and that was a relief.

It was shortly after New Year's, and Kyle and I had been together for about eight months. Everything was progressing well. The next Saturday night, I invited home to D.C. for the weekend. I cooked our favorite meal for dinner—fried chicken, baked macaroni and cheese, and spicy collard greens. It left both of us full and snuggled up together on the sofa watching television.

"Hey babe, I think I want to join the Air Force," Kyle blurted out.

At first, I was shocked and wasn't sure I'd heard him correctly.

"Huh? Where did that come from?" I turned toward him.

"I've just been thinking. I don't have room to grow where I'm at currently, and while the money is good, I just want to have more security. With my skills I can get a pretty good job in the military, as well as great benefits."

I was surprised. I thought Kyle was happy with his job. He was an IT supervisor at a call center. I had no clue he was thinking of changing careers, and I also knew that with him being in the military there might be times when we'd be away from each other for long periods of time.

"I've been talking to a recruiter, and I think it's a good idea."

"Well, whatever you want to do, I'll support you."

"You're mad, aren't you?" Kyle replied. "I can hear it in your voice."

While I wanted to be happy for him, I couldn't pretend like I wasn't disappointed. I liked the idea of security, but the thought of him leaving me, especially since our relationship was so new, had me worried.

"No, I'm not mad," I lied. I was pissed. I couldn't help but think I had wasted time, again. "I guess I'm just a little worried about whether things will change between us. What happens if you get stationed far away? I can't leave D.C. right now. You know I was offered a permanent position with the Attorney General's office. It's just a lot at one time, and we haven't been together that long. I don't want to ruin what we've built."

"So, will you marry me?"

His response caught me by surprise. He had to be joking, right? My heart fluttered with hope, but reality sank in. We had only briefly discussed marriage and if Jerell didn't want to get married after dating for two years, then I doubted Kyle wanted to after only eight months.

"Cut it out, Kyle. What do you mean 'will you marry me'? We've haven't even been dating a year yet."

Now I'm starting to sound like Jerell.

"I'm serious, Nakia. When we first met, I told you I don't have any trouble deciding what I want. Yes, we haven't been together for a long time, but I'm in love with you. I don't need any more time to know that you're the only woman I want to spend the rest of my life with."

I was speechless. My mind raced. *Was he really proposing to me? Were we ready for this? Was he my "Black Prince Charming?"* The more I thought about it, the more I realized I was getting exactly what I'd always wanted. Kyle was the one for me. I had asked God for a man to put a ring on it, and he was answering my prayers. So now that it was happening, it was no time to get cold feet.

Finally, after a few moments of silence, I responded. "Yes."

"Yes?"

"Yes, Kyle," I said choking back tears. "I'll marry you."

The smile on his face told me everything I needed to know.

Kyle truly loved me. While his proposal wasn't exactly what I had imagined it would be, all that really mattered to me in that moment was that I had a man who wanted to spend the rest of his life with me and I was about to get the one thing I'd always dreamed of: my *Black Prince Charming*.

CHAPTER 7

Time seemed to speed up after the proposal. Kyle had quit his job and moved in with me in D.C., so that we could spend more time together. There was no time to plan the big wedding that I'd always wanted because Kyle was planning to enlist in the Air Force in less than two weeks. Instead, we planned something short and sweet. While I told Toni and my mom about our plans, I didn't tell anyone else, including my father. I didn't want him to be upset that he couldn't walk me down the aisle.

Kyle and I married exactly one week after he proposed. We had decided to get married at the Justice of the Peace, but planned on having a bigger wedding after he was finished with boot camp and basic training.

As I stood in the bathroom at the courthouse, I looked at my reflection in the mirror. In an effort to look good on our special day, I had splurged on a strapless form fitting dress from White House Black Market. The dress hugged my curves and I was sure Kyle would love it, but somehow, I couldn't help but think about Jerell. *What was he doing? Had he hooked up with someone else in Europe?* I was sure he had. Every man has needs and I doubted he was thinking about me while he was in Europe, surrounded by other models. More importantly I started to understand Jerell's desire to wait until we were financially stable. He knew how important a big wedding was to me and all he wanted was to give me my dream. It was weird knowing that less than a year prior, I had been dreaming of marrying him. Things had changed so much since I'd met Kyle and I was beginning to wonder if I was moving too fast.

Everything just felt so rushed. However, since Kyle was leaving for boot camp so soon, we needed to have everything in place so that I was legally his wife before he enlisted. This would allow me the option to move with him once he was stationed.

After the Justice of Peace, we had a nice dinner at Georgia Brown's with Toni and one of Kyle's friends, and then went home. It honestly felt like just another day. It was not at all what I had imagined my wedding day to be. There was no big hoopla, no say-yes-to-the-dress moment, and no family there to support me. My mother did not attend, as to avoid my father from asking any questions about her whereabouts.

My heart ached that night, I loved Kyle, but it was hard to give up the wedding I had placed in my head for so long. Kyle had kept the secret from his family too, and I could tell he was upset that they hadn't been there. We stayed at the Mayflower hotel in D.C that night but there were no acrobatic sexcapades or hours of love making. We merely went through the motions of consummating our marriage and went to bed.

The day after we got married, I dropped Kyle off so he could complete the paperwork for the Air Force. I tried to keep myself busy with work and class so that I wouldn't think about my new husband being gone for more than a month, but I couldn't help but think about how much I'd miss him. Even in the short time that we'd been together, I'd become very close to him. We'd spent almost every free moment together since the weekend we'd met, so I knew life without him would feel empty.

On the night before Kyle was scheduled to leave for boot camp, I came home from work to an empty apartment. I was surprised because I had expected him to be there so I could cook him a nice dinner before he left in the morning. Figuring he'd be home any minute, I took a shower, and began dinner. Shortly after I started to cook, my phone rang. It was Kyle.

"Hey babe, where are you?" I asked.

"Hey, I'm at my dad's house. He wanted to spend some time with me before I left tomorrow, so I decided to stay in Richmond tonight. He'll give me a ride to the military processing center in the morning. I really wanted to see you, but my dad was really sad about me leaving so, you know how that goes."

I didn't know what to say. Kyle and I had never gotten into an argument before, but at that very moment, I wanted to smack the hell out of him. *Why would he think that spending that night at his father's house two hours away was okay, considering this was the last chance we'd have to see each other for six weeks.*

"Babe, are you there?"

"Yeah, I'm here. Honestly, Kyle, I don't know what to say. I'm not sure why you thought this was a good idea. It's your last night before boot camp, and now you're telling me I'm not going to see you until your graduation in six weeks? I'm not even going to get the chance to make love to my husband before he leaves me for boot camp, almost two-thousand miles away? I rushed home to cook you a nice dinner, and you're not even going to be here. This is crazy. Why couldn't you tell your dad, 'no'? You're a married man now, Kyle. That means I am your priority."

"I'm sorry, Nakia. To be honest with you, I was scared that if I spent my last night with you, I wouldn't be able to leave you in the morning."

"Are you kidding me?," I blurted.

"Look," he continued. "As soon as I'm situated, I'll write you. Before you know it, I'll see you at my graduation. I'm sorry this whole thing was rushed, and I wasn't able to give you the wedding you deserve with all of your family and friends, but I promise, as soon as this is all over, I'll make it up to you."

I sighed. There was nothing I could do. Kyle had made up his mind, and I'd just have to deal with it.

"Okay, Kyle. I love you. Make sure you write me as soon as you can so I can send you a care package. Stay strong, and I'll see you soon."

"I love you too baby. I'll see you soon."

When I hung up, I broke down and cried. This was not what I had expected the first week of marriage to be like. We hadn't even gotten a chance to go on a honeymoon. It was in that moment that I realized I might have made a big mistake.

It had been a week since Kyle had left and I still hadn't heard from him. I knew he mentioned it might be a while before he would be given a chance to write, but the hollowness in the pit of my stomach told me something was wrong. I tried to brush it off, telling myself I was tripping, but the feeling remained.

As I sat on the sofa watching TV one evening, my phone rang. I didn't recognize the number on the caller I.D. and got excited thinking it was Kyle.

"Hello?"

"Nakia? Is that you?" The voice on the other end was staticky, but decidedly male.

"Kyle?" I was so elated to hear from him I didn't know what to say.

There was a short silence and for a second, I thought I'd lost the call.

"No, Nakia, it's not *Kyle*," an irritated voice replied from the other end.

My heart sank when I recognized who I was talking to. "Hey, Jerell," I tried sounding casual and thought about how to make this any less awkward than it already was. "I'm sorry. I thought you were someone else."

"Why the fuck did you get married?"

I was frozen. Jerell had never talked to me like that. He'd never cursed at me or raised his voice, as far as I could remember.

"You couldn't do me the courtesy of breaking things off with me before running off with someone else? You know, I knew something was wrong when you returned from your trip, but when I got the gig in Europe, I'd hoped our time apart might strengthen our relationship, and make us realize how much we meant to each other. Instead, I call, and you don't answer. I leave messages, you don't respond. It's like you just moved on with your life and forgot to tell me. And then I find out that's exactly what you did. That's fucked up, Kia."

"Jerell, what did you expect? You left for a whole different country when our relationship was already in trouble. I just figured it was best for us to naturally grow apart. I'm sorry I didn't tell you I'd started seeing someone else. To be honest, I didn't know how to tell you that. I'm sorry how things happened, I'll take the blame for most of it, but our relationship was in trouble before I met Kyle."

"Fine, I can accept that Nakia, but married? You barely know this guy! Were you in that much of a rush to be someone's bride that you just settled for anything that came your way? I thought you were better than that?"

"Really, Jerell? You don't know a thing about my husband, so don't make assumptions."

"You don't know what I know about your husband."

"What is that supposed to mean?"

"It just means Richmond is small. Look, I'm sorry I went off on you. I was just really upset that I had to find out you were married from someone other than you. I don't have any ill will toward you, I'm just not sure I've gotten over you—or us. And now I have to deal with the fact that you've moved on and there won't be an 'us' anymore. It's just a lot." He sounded like his throat was constricting. "But I'll get over it. I take some of the blame too. I should've fought harder for us."

I felt terrible that I didn't do my part and end things the way I should've. Instead, I got caught up with Kyle and didn't think about Jerell's feelings. I was wrong, and I knew it.

"Jerell, I'm sorry things didn't work out for us. You're an amazing guy, and you were a wonderful boyfriend. Thank you for treating me like a queen. Because of you, I know how I should be treated by a man. I really wish you the best, and I know you'll find someone who will make you happy." When he didn't say anything—not that I thought he should've—I could no longer handle being on the phone with him. I felt like I had broken him, one of the kindest, most loyal men I'd ever known. "Look, Jerell, I gotta get going but—"

"It's cool. I just wanted to say that, if you ever need anything—I mean anything, Nakia—you call me. If that nigga ever hurts you in any way, call me. Okay?"

"Okay, Jerell. Thank you."

After hanging up, I felt even sadder. I was happy Jerell still cared about me and was willing to accept my apology, but I couldn't stop thinking about the fact that hearing his voice ignited a small flame in me. I still cared about him and that instilled more doubt about my marriage.

I couldn't stop thinking about Jerell's words. *What did he know about Kyle that I didn't? Was he just talking? Was I truly blind?* The worst part of it all was that I still hadn't heard from my husband. What had I gotten myself into?

CHAPTER 8

It was going on a month since Kyle had left, and I still hadn't heard from him. No call, no letter, nothing. My feelings had changed from worried to pissed. I Googled and called every military office I could find but no one seemed to know who Kyle was. Naïve to the recruitment process, I tried telling myself that since he was a new recruit his information wasn't in the system yet, but no matter what I used to reassure myself, something about the entire situation felt wrong. Very wrong.

It was a Saturday, and I was bored out of my mind. Most of my friends and family were in Virginia and I didn't hang out with colleagues or classmates much, so I had no one to spend time with in D.C. Deciding I needed a listening ear, I called Toni.

"Hey, friend. What are you up too?" I said attempting to sound upbeat.

"Hey, Mrs. Newlywed. Long time no speak. I've missed you, girl," she replied in a sincere tone.

"Yeah, I know. I've just been busy at work and what not. How have you been doing?"

"I'm doing okay. Just work, work, and more work. So, how's married life treating you? Did Kyle make it to boot camp in San Antonio okay?"

My upbeat tone was steadily declining. "Girl, I don't even know."

"What do you mean you don't know?" Toni shrieked.

I could no longer hide my worry. I was down and out, and my eyes began to well up with tears. "I mean I don't know. I haven't heard from him since the night before he left. I think something is wrong."

"You, think? Of course, something is wrong. You should have heard from him by now. I must be honest with you Nakia, I think you rushed into the whole marriage thing. Kyle is a good guy as far as I know, but I don't know of any man proposing to a woman after only eight months of dating. That was a red flag for me from the get-go."

My sadness turned to slight anger. "So, why didn't you say anything Toni? You're supposed to be my girl."

"Because you're hardheaded, and nothing I said would've made you change your mind with your crazy in-love self," I could hear her smirk through the phone. "You know I'm speaking truth," she said compassionately.

I laughed, because Toni was right. The only thing she

would've accomplished by saying something, would have been pissing me off.

"But seriously, Kia. Have you called his family? When my cousin went into the military, we heard from him within the first two weeks. Maybe his parents have heard from him."

"Why would he contact them but not me?"

"I don't know, Kia, but nothing about this sounds right. It's been a whole month since you've heard from him."

"Thanks for the reassurance, Toni."

"Look, I'm just being real. I really think you should call his parents. Didn't he and his dad live together? Maybe his dad has some mail at the house that has information about where he is."

"Girl, I don't even know if I have his dad's number. I never really needed it."

"You can always call directory assistance. You do know his name, right?"

"Yes, Toni, I know his father's name." Despite only having known Kyle for a few months, there were some things that every married person needed to know. "Wait! His dad's number should be on my caller ID. The night before Kyle left, he called me from the house." It was the first ray of hope I'd had in speaking to my husband all month. I couldn't wait any longer. "I'm going to call you back."

"Okay, girl. Let me know what happens."

"Okay, I will, bye."

My heart raced as I searched through the caller ID for the house number.

"Got it!"

I quickly dialed the number and took a deep breath as the phone rang.

An older man answered, his voice similar to Kyle's, but more distinguished. "Hello?"

"Hi, it's Nakia. I'm calling because I'm a little bit worried about Kyle."

"Worried? Why are you worried about Kyle?"

"Well, he told me he would contact me with his information as soon as he got settled in Texas, but I haven't heard from him, and it's been almost a month. I've called every recruiting office in the area, but no one seems to have any idea of who he is. I was wondering if you'd heard from him or received any mail from the Air Force that might tell me where he is?"

There was a short pause before Kyle's father spoke.

"Nakia, I don't know what's going on, but Kyle is sitting right here."

My heart pounded in my chest, and I began to feel faint.

After a few moments of processing what he had said, I responded. "He's where?"

"He's right here. Look, let me put him on the phone. I don't know what is going on and I don't want no parts of this mess."

At that moment, I felt more rage than I'd ever felt in my entire life. I wanted to kill Kyle. I couldn't think of one reason why he'd be at his father's, and whatever the reason was I knew it had better be good or I might just have ended up in jail that night.

After a few moments of muffled voices saying things I couldn't make out, Kyle got on the phone.

"Hey, babe."

"*Hey, babe?* Are you serious right now? You're just going to get on the phone and act like it's just a regular day. Kyle, what the hell is going on? Why aren't you in Texas!"

He sighed. "Nakia, look, I lied. I never joined the Air Force."

"What do you mean you never joined? I went with you to the recruiter's office and everything."

"Yeah, I know. I was thinking about it, but I never went back and signed the papers."

At that point, I was shaking. I didn't understand. *Who would lie about such a thing and why?*

"Listen, you're not making any sense to me right now. Why did you tell me you were joining the Air Force? You mean to tell me you've been at your dad's house all this time? I've been worried sick that something happened to you, and you've been chilling with your father? Are you for real right now?"

"Yes," he said calmly.

He was acting like it wasn't a big deal that he'd been lying to me for an entire month. I knew I should've trusted my instincts when I felt something was wrong. *Who the hell did I marry?*

"Kyle, I'm going to need more than these one-word answers you're giving me. Why would you lie to me about something like this? Just be real. Is there someone else? Are you living a double life?"

"No, Nakia. It's nothing like that."

"So, what the hell is it then?"

He took a deep breath. "When I told you I had quit my job, I had actually been fired."

"Okay, and?" I replied impatiently.

"Well, you had been doing so well in your career, I guess I just couldn't deal with the fact that you would be making all that money. I was broke and unemployed. I couldn't deal with that. So, I figured I'd join the military, and I'd be someone you could be proud to be with. But, I'm a bad test-taker and I didn't score high enough on the ASVAB test, so I knew right away the Air Force wasn't in the cards for me."

"Okay, but I still don't get why you thought lying to me was the answer. Are you crazy?"

"I was embarrassed about the test. I didn't want you to think I was a failure. So, I made up the whole thing about leaving for boot camp. I asked you to marry me because I didn't want to lose you. I figured you'd be more willing to hear me out as my wife as opposed to just my girlfriend. I wanted to tell you, but the longer the lie went on, the harder it was for me to face you with the truth. Listen, I'm truly sorry. I fucked up big time, I know."

I couldn't believe what I was hearing. I was married to a freaking *decepticon*, a "representative." If I wasn't sure before, I definitely knew at that point that I'd made a huge mistake by marrying him. I was hurt and embarrassed. How could I tell my family and friends what happened? I still hadn't even told my dad we were married. How could Kyle do this to me? I felt sick to my stomach. He had made an utter fool out of me.

"Kyle, I have to go." I said abruptly, not sure I could keep the contents of my stomach down. "I can't talk to you right now. I need time to get my thoughts together."

I hung up the phone. I didn't even give him a chance to respond, afraid I'd only hear more lies.

He called me back ten times before realizing I wouldn't answer. I lay in bed that night and cried. How foolish was I? How did I get so caught up? I was so ashamed. My parents raised me better than that. My father would've never done something like that to my mother. Everything began to hit me at once, and I couldn't help but wonder what else he'd lied to me about.

CHAPTER 9

I couldn't move from my spot in the bed for over an hour. After back-to-back missed calls from Kyle—and a few more from Toni —I disconnected the phone. At some point, I must have fallen asleep because I was awakened around midnight by loud knocking on my apartment door. Half asleep, I walked to the front door and looked through the peephole.

I was hardly surprised to see Kyle because who else would be at my door that late? But he looked different. He had a desperate look in his eyes.

I put the chain on and cracked the door open.

"What do you want, Kyle?"

"Nakia, please let me in. I'm sorry. I really need to talk to you."

His eyes were bloodshot like he'd been crying.

I told you I needed time to think. Just go back to Richmond. I'll call you later today."

"No, Kia. Please. I fucked up. I get it. Please. I don't want to lose you over this."

"Well, maybe you should've thought about all that before you put me through this unnecessary bull. Like, what did I do to deserve any of this? Do you know how I feel right now?"

All he could do was hang his head down in shame, and it pissed me off even more.

"I've already contacted a lawyer to have our marriage annulled." Now I was the one doing the lying, but he deserved it as far as I was concerned. "I can't be putting up with this foolishness. I'm too grown for this mess."

Kyle jumped and stood closer to the door. "Nakia, please don't. I promise I'll never lie to you again. I was so worried about what you would think of me after I lost my job. I wasn't thinking clearly. I promise I'll make it up to you." Tears began to pour from his eyes. "Please open the door, so we can talk. I need you, Nakia. I can't bear being without you."

No man had ever cried for me. I hated seeing him like that —or rather, I guess I kind of liked it. To see him in so much pain was proof that I meant something to him. Even if he was an idiot who'd lied to me for a month, at least he had done it because he cared about what I thought about him. Reluctantly, I opened the door and let him in. Besides, I didn't want my neighbors knowing all of my business.

After we were seated across from each other at my kitchen table, Kyle began to talk.

"I'm just going to tell you everything."

"Wow, and here I thought you'd already told me everything," I replied, rolling my eyes.

"Go ahead. Say what you have to say."

He took a deep breath before speaking. "Before I got fired, my manager called me into his office. A few computers and laptops had gone missing from the storage room, and it happened during my shift."

"You got caught stealing computers? What are you? On drugs?"

"No, hell no! I didn't steal anything and I'm not on drugs. The truth is, I fucked up. Mark, one of my team members, had just enrolled in college and asked if he could borrow a computer for a few weeks so he could do some schoolwork. He said he'd return it once he had enough money to buy his own. The computers were just sitting in the storage room collecting dust, so I let him. I gave him the key to the storage room and let him pick one of them for himself, and that was that. I didn't think anything else about it. But then I get an email that six of the computers had gone missing and that there was an active investigation into their whereabouts.

"I immediately called Mark, but his phone was disconnected. I asked a few of the other team members if they'd seen him, and one of them told me they'd heard he'd up and quit without turning in a notice. I was surprised because I hadn't heard anything about it.

"So, at this point I'm pissed. Later that afternoon, I get called into my manager's office. Apparently, they got a call from Henrico County Police Department that the computers had been pawned by Mark. They also had me on surveillance handing him the keys to the storage room, and so as far as they were concerned, I was complicit in the theft. They fired me on the spot. I got a notice to appear in court, but it was sent to my dad's address. Because I had been staying with you at the time I never got it. Since I didn't appear in court, I now have a warrant out for my arrest, but no one has come by to arrest me yet. I've basically been at the crib ever since, hiding out."

I was flabbergasted. I couldn't believe what I'd just been told. I was unable to think rationally. Who the hell was I in a relationship with? Not only was my husband a *decepticon* suffering from a severe case of *lieabetes*, he was also a wanted criminal. I didn't even know how to process the information he was giving me.

I began to hyperventilate. Kyle rushed to my side and wrapped me in his arms until I calmed down.

"I'm so sorry, Kia. I never meant to put you through any of this. I promise I'll make things right, baby. Please. I need you to tell me you forgive me."

As much as I wanted to tell him "no" and call a lawyer for real to start the annulment process, all I kept hearing in the back of my head was our wedding vows, "for better or worse."

I'd asked God for a man to marry me and I'd gotten just that. Unfortunately for me, I was being forced to eat my words.

"I don't know, Kyle. I love you, but what you did really hurt me."

"Let me make it up to you. It was never my intention to hurt you. Again, babe, I'm sorry."

I didn't say a word. I sat there numb. The idea of forgiving him was hard to justify but I loved him. *Love conquers all —doesn't it?*

Kyle must have taken my silence for forgiveness because the next thing I knew his head was between my thighs. As he kissed and licked passionately between my legs, I wanted to tell him to stop, but I was so frustrated and missed his touch, I let him continue until I orgasmed. Then, he led me to the bedroom where he made love to me over and over until I had no choice but to forgive him. Honestly, Kyle knew my body better than anyone, and his love had become my weakness. I just couldn't resist him, and that was the problem.

CHAPTER 10

Over the next couple of weeks, Kyle did everything he could to prove himself to me. Toni hooked him up with an under-the-table job doing security at one of her friend's night clubs in D.C. He spent all of his time either at work, the gym, or in our apartment. The plan was for him to earn enough money for bail and lawyer fees before turning himself in. So far, the cops hadn't caught up with him, so he was doing his best to make sure he had enough money before they did. I told him, under no circumstances would I be paying for his mistakes, and he assured me he'd earn the money himself.

One evening, as I walked into our apartment from a long day at work, my phone rang. I answered and an automated voice informed me I had a collect call from the Henrico County Jail. It was Kyle. My heart froze but I accepted the charges.

"Kia, I'm so sorry. I got pulled over on the way to the gym for failure to stop at a stop sign, and when they ran my name, all of my warrants came up."

"*All* of your warrants? I thought you only had one warrant, Kyle? What the hell are you talking about, and what am I supposed to do about this?"

"Well, they transported me to Richmond, and I have a bail hearing tomorrow. I was hoping you could come to bail me out?"

"Oh, hell no. I am not paying your way out of this. You fucked up, so now you deal with the consequences."

"Okay, well, can you just come to show your support? I don't have much time left on this call, but I hope you can come. I love you, Kia."

The call disconnected.

I was pissed, and I wanted to know what Kyle meant by "warrants." I immediately got on my computer and did a background search. After paying a fee for the results, I couldn't believe what I saw. Not only did Kyle have a warrant out for his arrest for fraud, but he also had a laundry list of warrants that ranged from DUIs, possession of marijuana, and failures to appear in court. This was not the man I thought I'd married. This was not the kind of man I wanted to be with. I knew right then that I needed to figure out how to end things as soon as possible.

～

I needed to hear the real story regarding his charges, so against my better judgment, I called off from work and drove to Kyle's hearing the next morning. The courthouse was packed, and I had no clue what courtroom he was in. I waited in line at the information desk and I noticed two girls standing in front of me. When it was their turn at the desk, I was surprised to hear one of the women mention Kyle's name. At first, I thought I was tripping, but after they spelled out his last name, I knew I'd heard correctly. I left the line and followed them down the hallway to the room where Kyle was. I sat silently in the back watching everything that was going on. Kyle had several charges, and he would have to pay ten thousand dollars bail. I sucked my teeth. There was no way in hell I was paying that for him.

Once the hearing was over, I walked over to the women, that were in line at the information desk.

"Hi, I'm Nakia. Kyle's wife. I overheard you mention his name at the information desk, and I'm just wondering how you know him?"

They exchanged confused glances before one of them responded.

"Kyle asked us to come here to help him with bail. We both dated him a while back."

"Let me get this straight. Both of you used to date Kyle, and you both plan on paying his bail?" There is no way in hell they would pay his bail unless there was something else going on. "Are either of you still messing with him?"

"No, it's nothing like that. Kyle is just a good guy. Neither of us knew each other before last night, but he put us in contact with each other, and we were able to come up with five thousand a piece."

"Okay, forgive me if I'm not understanding, but why would you do this for a man you're not with?"

"Like she said," the other woman responded. "Kyle is just a good guy. Back when we dated, he helped me out a lot with my daughter. I figured I owed it to him. Plus, I know he'll pay me back when he can."

I couldn't believe what I was hearing. Two women that Kyle no longer had any ties to were willing to give a substantial amount of money to get him out of jail. Unbelievable. All I could do was shake my head in disbelief as I walked out of the courthouse.

"Well, better them than me," I said before getting into my car.

I sat behind the wheel, thinking of everything that had transpired, and I decided that I would call the lawyer as soon as I got back to D.C. An annulment couldn't come soon enough. There was just too much drama with my husband, and I was over it.

Before heading home, I decided to stop by my parent's house. I hadn't seen them since before I got married, and I really missed them. As soon as I walked in the house, I was greeted by a huge smile from my mom.

"Hey, mom." I walked over to give her a kiss and a hug.

"Hey, baby. I missed you. How have you been?"

I had no intentions of discussing my issues with Kyle with her. But I could tell by the way she was looking at me that she knew something was wrong. I was hoping that she hadn't heard about him somehow.

"I've been okay, ma'. Just busy at work, that's all. How are you and daddy? Where is he, anyway?"

"Oh, your dad went out to run a few errands, but we've been good. I've just been wondering when I'd hear from you. The last time we talked, you were getting married and I was a bit disappointed not being able to be there, but I figured you'd come around to see us at some point."

That was my mom. Protective, but willing to give me space. Both of my parents were like that. I was the only child, so of course they worried, but they felt as though they'd raised me well enough to be able to handle my own problems, so they rarely interfered in my private affairs.

Once my dad returned, I hung out with my parents for the rest of the day, watching movies and making small talk. Both were retired, so they loved when I took the time to spend a day with them.

I listened as they told me about things going on at our church and about an upcoming vacation they were planning, and it was about nine-thirty that night before I realized how much time had passed.

"Why don't you stay the night in your old room, Kia? It's too late for you to be driving back to D.C. by yourself," my dad said, as he caught me yawning on the couch.

I was exhausted and it felt good to be in the comfort of my childhood home, away from the responsibilities of being a grown up. "Yeah, I think I will. I'll just have to leave early in the morning." I hated the idea of being late especially since I had accepted that permanent position with the Attorney General's Office. I was an assistant to an attorney and did not want to mess up my chances of being an attorney there one day myself. "So, I can make it somewhat on time for work."

Despite everything that had happened that day, I slept like a baby that night.

I left my parent's house a little before dawn the next morning. I walked into our apartment and jumped when I saw Kyle sitting on the living room couch.

"Damn, Kyle. I didn't even see your car out in the parking lot."

"Is it a problem that I'm here?" he asked calmly.

Honestly, I didn't want him there. His presence was not comforting and felt awkward. "No," I lied. "I just didn't expect to see you."

"So, where have you been? I've been waiting for you all night. You didn't think to call me?"

"This coming from the man who disappeared for a month! First off, Kyle, I had no clue you were getting out yesterday. As far as where I've been, it doesn't feel so good to not know where someone you care about is, does it?"

Kyle sighed. "With all that I have done, I will let it go. I was just worried about you. I thought something had happened to you. Why didn't you stick around after the hearing?"

"I don't know. I figured you needed to spend time with your *girlfriends* to thank them for bailing you out."

"Very funny. Shay and Yvette are not my girlfriends." He squinted, sitting straighter in the couch. "Is that why you left? They told me ya'll met when I got out. Nothing is going on between me and either one of them, they're just good people."

"I see."

"What's that supposed to mean?"

"Nothing. Look, I have to get ready for work. I'm already running late. We'll talk about this later," I said before heading to the bedroom.

As soon as I walked into my office, I was bombarded with work. I barely had time for a break. Combine that with the stress of everything that was going on with Kyle, and by the end of the day, I had the most terrible headache. I'm not much of a drinker, but that night I knew I'd need one.

A few of my coworkers were heading to a local bar for

happy hour and invited me to go with them. For the first time ever, I agreed. My talk with Kyle would just have to wait. Besides, it was about time he got a taste of his own medicine.

The bar was crowded, and we barely found seats together. As I took a few shots and shared some appetizers with my colleagues, I watched as they took turns singing karaoke. Something about being in the bar made me miss being single, and I regretted rushing into marriage with Kyle. I wanted my life back. I was tired of being stressed out, wondering what new revelation I'd find out about the man I married but barely knew.

But, no matter how much my brain told me to free myself from Kyle, my heart wasn't sure I'd be able to.

I arrived back at my apartment around nine that night. Once again, Kyle was sitting on the sofa, waiting.

I had barely gotten through the door before he whipped around to face me. "So, we're about to make this a regular thing, I see?"

"Don't start. I have a headache."

He stood up. "Where were you, Nakia?"

"Out, Kyle. I was out. Why?"

"Why? Because you're my wife and I think I should know where you're at."

The nerve of him asking me about my whereabouts. I rolled my eyes, walked away, and mumbled. "Not for long..."

"Not for long? What does that mean?"

"It means that it's time to let this go. I don't want to go

through this anymore. I can't keep sacrificing my happiness. All this stuff you got going on is way too much."

"I know it's a lot, Kia, but what about for better or for worse?"

"Don't do that, Kyle. Don't use those words against me like our marriage isn't already built on lie."

Kyle walked over and stood in front of me, cornering me in the kitchen. Though he was at least a foot and a half taller than me, he looked me right in the eyes. "So, are you saying this isn't real?" His tone was low and sexual.

I could feel his breath against my face, and those familiar tingles began to travel throughout my body. I did not want to give in, but the intensity of his gaze excited me. As much as I knew ending things was the right thing for me to do, I couldn't deny the sexual hold he had over me.

Before I could say a word, Kyle pinned me up against the wall. His teeth dug into my neck as he pulled up my skirt. I felt my wetness slide down my inner thighs and legs as my panties dropped down to my ankles. I grabbed the back of his neck and kissed him passionately as he lifted one of my legs and grabbed my thigh and ass aggressively.

In one swift motion he turned me around toward the wall and entered me from behind.

I braced myself against the wall as he stroked fervently while grabbing one of my breasts with one hand and rubbing my clit with the other. Every emotion I'd had, poured out as I moaned with pleasure.

My legs began to quiver as I reached my climax, and as I whined his name, I knew at that moment that letting him go wouldn't be easy. In fact, it would be damn near impossible. He may have had a bad case of *lieabetes*, but there was no denying I had *Kylebetes*.

CHAPTER 11

It was two days before Kyle's trial for the fraud case, and needless to say, the both of us were on edge. His lawyer advised that, if found guilty, he'd do two years at a minimum. Luckily, his lawyer was able to settle his other charges with fines and no jail time. All we could do at that point was hope that he would beat the case.

Kyle swore to me that he was innocent and that he'd simply used bad judgment when he let his team member borrow the computer. I believed him, so I caved and helped him get his lawyer.

We'd decided to call it an early night, but while Kyle slept peacefully next to me, I couldn't help but think about the possibility of becoming an inmate's wife. This had never been in the plans for me. *What happened to meeting my "Black Prince Charming," getting swept up off my feet, and living happily ever after?* Nothing in my life was going as planned, and no matter how I tried to free myself from Kyle, something about him made it hard for me to let him go.

The next morning, Kyle and I drove to Richmond to spend the night at his father's before the trial. A few of his family members stopped by to lend their support, and the evening was filled with food and drinks. Everyone insisted that Kyle would beat the case. I hoped they were right.

It was about 9:00 p.m., and everyone had left. Kyle was in the shower, and his father had gone out for drinks with one of his friends, so Kyle and I were the only ones in the house. As I lay on the couch, half-thinking, half-watching TV, the doorbell rang. I yelled for Kyle, but remembered he was in the shower, so I went to answer it myself.

When I opened the door, I was surprised to see a woman, about my age, standing there with a small child.

"Hi, may I help you?"

"Yes, I'm here to see Kyle."

Right away alarm bells began ringing in my head. *Oh, boy. What is this about?*

"Kyle!" I yelled toward the bathroom before letting the woman in and offering her a seat. Then I marched to the bathroom and pushed open the door.

"Kyle!"

"Yo!" Kyle said as he peeked from behind the shower curtain. "What's up?"

"Some girl with a child is here to see you," I said, before rolling my eyes, and turning to walk back into the living room.

The girl was taller and a thicker build than me. She appeared to be biracial. She was pretty. The little boy sitting on her lap was cute. He was a medium brown complexion with low cut wavy hair, and he was about two years old.

"I'm sorry, I didn't catch your name," I said to the woman.

"Oh, I'm sorry. My name is Tamika. Are you Kyle's sister?"

"No," I had to fight back my rage at the suggestion. "My name is Nakia. I'm his wife."

The woman looked stunned.

"I'm so sorry. I didn't know he was married."

"Yeah, I hear that a lot."

Kyle walked into the living room wearing sweats.

I caught Tamika gazing at him, and she quickly turned away when she noticed me looking at her.

"Tamika? What are you doing here?"

"I don't know how to say this, and I promise I didn't come here to start any trouble, but there's something I need to tell you."

I immediately felt sick. I already knew what she was going to say before she said it. "Okay," Kyle said, looking naïve to the fact that a child was with her.

"I'm just going to say it. This is my son, Kyle Jr., and you're his father."

Even though I already had suspicions, hearing her say those

words was far worse than I could have imagined. My legs felt weak, so I walked to the other side of the room to grab a seat.

"You can't be serious. It was just one night a long ass time ago. That boy has to be like two years old Tamika. Why are you just telling me this now?"

She shrugged. "I don't know. I was pissed at how abruptly you ended things. We had a one-night stand, and I was embarrassed. I figured I could take care of him by myself. My mother has been helping me out, but she recently got sick and can't help me financially anymore. I can't take care of him alone."

"Wow. So, basically the only reason why you've decided to tell me about *my* son is that you need money? Well, I have news for you. I don't have any money. Tomorrow I'm going to court on a theft charge, and if I'm found guilty, I'm going away for a while, so you really picked a bad time to give me this news."

I was barely paying attention to the conversation. All I could do was look at the little boy. He had almond-shaped eyes, small ears, the cutest button nose—he looked just like Kyle. As I stared at him, I realized with deep resentment that I wouldn't be the first woman to give my husband a child. I felt like shit, and all I kept hearing in the back of my head were the words "divorce him."

As Kyle and Tamika talked, I left the room and went to Kyle's old bedroom. They needed to be alone and so did I. I couldn't believe how drastically my life had changed in such a short amount of time. In less than eighteen months I had married a pathological liar and potential criminal who had a two-year-old son. How could my life be so horrible? The only thing good I'd received out of our relationship was bomb sex. All I could do was shake my head.

An hour later, Kyle walked into the bedroom.

He was distraught. "I know you're tired of me telling you I'm sorry, but I swear I didn't know anything about that child."

I was silent.

"Kia, say something. I know you're angry, but I can't tell you about something I didn't know. I'm just as pissed as you are. I'm facing jail time, and now I have to deal with the fact that I have a two-year-old kid and I'm in no position to help take care of him."

"So, what are you going to do? Do you believe her?" I asked, even though I had no doubt that it was his son. I guess I was still hoping it wasn't true.

"Yeah, I do. We talked and the timing matches up, and I'm not gonna lie, the kid looks like me."

"Yeah, I know."

"I want to be in his life, Nakia. I'm no deadbeat. As soon as this case is straightened out, I'm going to get my shit together. But I need you in my life too. I can't do any of this without you."

I wanted to tell him, "No, I won't be there for you," but deep down in my heart, I knew I would. Win or lose, I was going to stick by my man's side. While I wasn't going to give that woman any money, I would do what I could to make sure I was a good stepmother. Besides, the child was part of Kyle, and Kyle was still my husband.

After telling Kyle that I would be there for him and that I would help raise his son, we went to bed. While he slept soundlessly, I tossed and turned all night. I was a stepmom now.

After a three-day trial, we were at the courthouse awaiting the verdict. Kyle was covered in sweat and wouldn't stop fidgeting.

The bailiff handed the judge the verdict. I took a deep breath. My legs were shaking as I braced myself for the news.

"Guilty."

I didn't want to believe what I'd just heard. While I knew the evidence against Kyle was strong, I was still hoping that everything would be okay. But it wasn't. With my husband being convicted of grand larceny, my worst nightmare had just come true: I was now the wife of a felon.

As Kyle's father drove us back to his house, the car was silent. Sentencing was scheduled for a week later, and Kyle was ordered to stay in Virginia during the week before sentencing. Kyle did his best to get his affairs in order. He took a paternity test and confirmed what we already knew. His family threw him a going away party and Kyle invited Tamika over to introduce Kyle Jr. to the family.

After a long week of preparing for sentencing, I was mentally exhausted. My mind, body, and soul were numb from everything I was going through. All I wanted to do was take a nice hot bath and forget everything, even for just an hour.

I relaxed in the bubble bath and thought about everything that had happened since I'd met Kyle. Cheating on Jerell, Kyle's lies about the Air Force, the stolen computers, the warrants, the secret child; my life was a hot mess. As I reflected nausea overcame me. Thinking I was feeling sick from the heat in the bathtub, I decided to run a little bit of cold water to cool off, but it wasn't helping. My head was spinning, and I began to wonder if it was something I ate during the party. When my vision stated to blur, I stumbled out of the tub and toward the door to call for Kyle. But before I could reach it, everything went black.

I woke up to beeping noises and the smell of rubbing alcohol. As my vision adjusted, I noticed Kyle staring down at me with a worried expression.

"What happened?" I asked, recognizing I was in a hospital.

"You passed out in the bathroom," Kyle replied.

"Damn," I managed, still feeling a little groggy. "I wonder why?"

"I don't know. The doctor should be back in here shortly with some answers. All I know is you scared the hell out of me. I thought I was going to lose you," Kyle said, tears forming in his eyes.

"Well, I have good news for you," the doctor said, entering the room. "You're going to be okay. It looks like you're just a little dehydrated, so I've ordered some fluids, and you should be back to normal in a few hours."

"Thank goodness," Kyle breathed in relief.

"We have to finish your paperwork, so I will need to ask you a few more questions. Do you already have an OB-GYN picked out?" the doctor asked nonchalantly.

"What does an OB-GYN have to do with dehydration," I asked impatiently.

"Well Mrs. Brown, you're pregnant. I'm sorry, I assumed the nurse told you. You're three weeks along."

This can't be right. Pregnant? Me? Now?

I was released from the hospital a few hours later. As we rode home, Kyle was deep in thought, and I was too shocked to say anything. After we were back in his bedroom, he finally spoke.

"So, we're having a baby?" Kyle said slowly with an unsure tone.

I sighed in disappointment. "Yeah, it seems that way."

Kyle stared at me for a moment before asking, "Are you going to be all right? I mean, obviously, this is not what I planned for us. You know that, right?"

"Yeah. I guess I'll have to be all right. What else can I do?" I replied with an annoyed tone.

"Nakia, I'm so sorry. I hate the idea of you going through our first pregnancy alone. I want to be there for you through it all. I want to be there when our child's born. It's already bad that I wasn't there when Kyle Jr. was born. I really messed everything up. I don't think I'll ever forgive myself."

I didn't have much of a response for him. I was still processing everything. All I wanted was go to sleep, so, that is exactly what I did.

The next morning we arrived bright and early at the courthouse. As his wife, I was given the opportunity to speak on Kyle's behalf. I mentioned that I'd just found out I was pregnant and that it would be a grave disservice if he were sentenced to a long period of time. In the end, the judge was a little lenient because Kyle was only sentenced to eighteen months. I don't know if it was pregnancy hormones or the fact that I was just overall heartbroken, but I began to cry right there in the courtroom.

Kyle managed to give me a quick hug and a kiss before he was led away by the bailiff. My heart broke into a billion pieces. I didn't know how I was going to get through this all alone.

Later that night, as I lay in bed alone, all I could think about was all the mistakes I'd made. How could I allow myself to make such stupid choices? I really had to get my shit together because I had more than just me to think about now. From that moment forward, I decided to think like a mother. I could no longer let my sexual needs influence my decisions.

It was time for me to act like a grown-up, and deep down I knew that meant divorcing Kyle.

CHAPTER 12

ONE MONTH LATER

"Thank you for calling the office of Smith and Lang. My name is Laurie. How may I help you?" a friendly, high-pitched voice asked.

"Hello, my name is Nakia Brown, and I am interested in getting information on the annulment process." I replied in an eager but professional tone.

"I would be more than happy to help you with that. Let me advise you on the difference between an annulment and divorce. An annulment means that the marriage is null and void or simply put, never happened. Whereas divorce ends a legal marriage. I can ask you a series of questions to see I you qualify for an annulment, if you'd like?"

My ears perked up. *Qualify?* "Yes, please."

"According to the law in the District of Columbia you must meet one of the following criteria. At the time of marriage, were you and or your spouse mentally incapacitated?"

With my hasty decision to marry Kyle, mental incapacitation may be an option. "No," I answered.

"Under the age of sixteen?"

Only a teenager would have made the decision to marry him so quickly. "No."

"Legally married to someone else?"

Goodness, if only I had waited and married Jerell I would not be in this predicament. "No."

"Close relatives?"

Humph, not even close. No one in my family is that damn crazy. "No."

"Married due to force or fraud?"

Could this be my out? This time, I thought for a moment before speaking.

"Mrs. Brown, are you still there?"

"Yes, I am. If my husband lied to me about going into the military in order for us to get married, would that qualify as fraud?" I replied in an anxious tone.

"In order to meet the criteria for force, he would have had to threaten you with violence." *Nope that wouldn't work.* I sighed.

"To qualify under the fraud provision, he would have had to have misrepresented or concealed pertinent information essential to the marr—"

"Bingo!" I shouted cutting her off.

"Glad I was able to find a potential option for you. You will need to speak with an attorney to get further information as I am just a paralegal. May I have the best contact number for you, Mrs. Brown?"

I was so excited I quickly blurted out my phone number and had to repeat it again. "Thank you so much for your help, Laurie."

"No problem. One of our attorneys will contact you in the next twenty-four to forty-eight hours."

"Thanks again," I said before hanging up.

A month had passed since Kyle had gone to jail and I hadn't really overcome the shock of it all. After talking to the attorney's office, I finally felt like things were moving in the right direction. I still had doubts about the annulment every now and then, but I kept myself busy with work to move those thoughts to the backburner. Still, every night as I lay in bed, I couldn't help but wonder if I was simply being tested by God. I was seven weeks pregnant and I hadn't told a soul. The only other person who knew was Kyle's dad, and while I was happy to be pregnant, I didn't think about it as much as I probably should have. I was too busy working, attending night classes, or in the apartment sleeping. However, I made it a point to visit Kyle on the weekends. Per Kyle's request, I even brought Kyle Jr. to visit him a couple of times. While I wasn't sure how I felt about bringing a child to a jail, both Kyle and Tamika were okay with it, so I didn't voice my concerns.

Being a stepmother gave me an idea of what was coming,

however, I still actively avoided thinking about my pregnancy. I didn't schedule any prenatal appointments right away. I didn't scribble down potential baby names. I really couldn't bring myself to do any of it. I was numb. And while I was excited to become a mom, I couldn't bask in my happiness the way I'd wanted to with Kyle gone. I wanted him to be there to share in the excitement and plan for our baby. I wanted things to be the way they *should* be.

I don't know why I was upset though. Nothing about our relationship up until that point had been the way it should've been.

It was a Friday night and I was exhausted. I had a busy week at work, and all I wanted to do was sleep until Monday morning. I cooked up my favorite dinner, the same one I'd always made for Kyle and I—fried chicken, spicy collard greens, and some baked macaroni and cheese—and had just finished eating. I had plans to visit Kyle the next morning, and while he enjoyed our visits, I really didn't feel like going. I was getting cold feet on proceeding with the annulment process and the idea of being a single mother. I just needed to sleep and get my mind off of things.

I showered and, with no plans of leaving the house, threw on a tank top and panties. After throwing some clothes in the wash, I settled on my sofa to catch up on some television and eventually I dozed off. I woke up with the most excruciating pain I'd ever felt in my abdomen. The pain was worse than menstrual cramping. It felt like my insides were being rung out like a wet t-shirt. There was a sticky wetness between my legs. I reached for the light and immediately knew something was wrong as blood had soaked through my panties and the sofa cushions beneath me. I immediately began to panic and sob as I feared the worst for my baby. I managed to make it to the bathroom as blood continued to gush heavily from my body. The pain seemed to get worse as I walked. I was convinced my uterus was tying itself up in a knot.

I was scared as hell. Rather than calling nine-one-one and waiting for an ambulance, I changed my clothes and put on as many pads as possible to catch the bleeding. I sobbed and prayed as I drove myself to the emergency room.

I wanted my baby to be okay, but I couldn't help but wonder if I'd been cursed. Ever since I'd met Kyle, nothing had gone right.

I arrived at the hospital and luckily, the Emergency Room wasn't busy, so I was seen within minutes. After speaking with a nurse and getting bloodwork done, I had an ultrasound. Afterwards, the doctor came into my room to confirm what I already knew.

"Mrs. Brown, you are having a miscarriage," the doctor said while rubbing my back to console me.

I continued to sob as my worst fear was confirmed.

"I'm so sorry this is happening. Is there anyone I can call to be with you?" the doctor asked.

I shook my head, trying to regain my composure. "No, I'll be okay."

I was advised to take Tylenol for the pain and to schedule an appointment with a gynecologist in a week. The nurse also gave me a pamphlet explaining what I should expect since the miscarrying process could take a few days, and a note excusing me from work and class for a few days.

I left the hospital a few hours later and I couldn't help but feel defeated. I knew Kyle had a lot to do with my miscarriage but maybe I had caused it too. I should have cared sooner. I should have done more. My life was completely unraveling. My unborn child paid for my mistakes. It was as if I was so focused on all the drama that I lost sight of the life forming inside of me. My hasty decisions had me dealing with the most traumatic experience of my life.

As I sat in the driver's seat, I could see the sun begin to rise on the horizon. As glimmers of a new day began to shine through, I coped with the fact that motherhood was not in the cards for me right now and that maybe it was for the best. Bringing a child into all of this turmoil was so not going to make things any better. As much as I was hurting, I knew deep down that everything happened for a reason, and though I wanted to be a mother, the timing was all wrong. Before pulling off, I said a silent prayer to God to keep my unborn child safe, and for the opportunity to become a mother later when the timing was right.

Then I drove home to my empty apartment.

Later that day, I was awoken from a nap by my phone ringing. I glanced at the caller ID and saw that it was Kyle. With everything that had happened I'd forgotten I was supposed to visit him.

"Hey, babe. Why didn't you come see me?" he asked after I accepted his call.

"Hey, I'm sorry. I—I couldn't make it today. I'm," I wanted to tell him; I knew he deserved to know, but I didn't have the strength to revisit that pain yet. "I'm not feeling well."

"What's wrong Nakia? Is it the baby?"

There was a pause before I spoke. "Yeah—" I struggled to find the words to tell him I'd miscarried. I could feel a huge knot forming in my throat as tears brimmed at my eyelids.

"What is it, Nakia? What happened?" Kyle asked, concerned.

"I had to go to the hospital last night. The baby is gone. I'm miscarrying."

My sadness quickly turned into anger. There I was, in an empty apartment as I miscarried my first child while my husband was hours away in jail of all places. I wanted to hit him until he felt the pain I was feeling. I was not a doctor, but I was convinced the stress of everything with Kyle had played a role in the miscarriage.

"This is all your fucking fault! You should be here with me right now, Kyle. Instead, you're in a fucking jail cell, while I'm here all alone, bleeding and in pain. Do you have any clue how fucked up I feel right now? I don't deserve this shit, Kyle! This is not how a marriage is supposed to be! I'm so ready to complete the paper work and be done with you. I don't have time to waste on someone who constantly lies to me. I don't have time to waste on a man who I can't depend on, who continues to feed me empty promises. I'm tired of you telling me you're sorry. I'm tired of working my ass off all week and then having to drive up to see you in jail every damn weekend. I'm just tired of it all! But most importantly, I'm tired of being a single fucking wife!"

The relief that came over me after I said everything I'd been holding in for the past couple of months was refreshing. I was tired of pretending like I was the happy, ride-or-die wife. I didn't want to be a rider to a man who couldn't return the favor. The more I reflected on my relationship with Kyle the more it was becoming clear that, while I'd given my all to him, the only thing he'd given me was stress and good dick—and that wasn't enough anymore.

"Nakia, I'm so—I mean, I know you're upset. I wish I were there to be with you. I wish I were there to hug you and kiss you and make everything all right. It kills me that you're going through this alone, and I know you don't want to hear this, but I am sorry. I'd give everything to change all of this and make different decisions. But it doesn't work like that, and as much as you are hurting right now, I hurt as well."

I couldn't help but roll my eyes. How many apologies had this man given me since we'd been together?

"Nakia, I love you, and I loved our baby. I'd give the world to change how all of this turned out. I'm so sorry, baby. All I can ask is that you forgive me and give me the opportunity to make it up to you. I know I don't deserve it, but I'm asking for you to have compassion. I can't live my life without you."

I was suddenly reminded of the women who helped me pay his bail. "Hmm, it seems like you did just fine before you met me, Mr. Lady's Man."

"And not one of them are in my life today. Are you really telling me you have no clue how much you mean to me? How special you are?"

"I really do wonder sometimes, Kyle. A man who truly loved me like you say you do wouldn't continue to hurt me like you have. He wouldn't lie to me for no reason."

"Damn, woman. What do I have to do to show you that you are the most important person in my life? I'll be honest, before I met you, I had any woman I wanted, but it was never more than sex. The moment I laid eyes on you in that van, I felt electricity soar through my body, something that no other woman has ever made me feel. It was like I was connected to you without knowing anything about you. I knew then that you'd be my wife."

I was silent. Kyle was good at saying all the right things, he always had been. I was determined not to be fooled by his charm, but the sincerity in his voice made me consider what he was saying. *Maybe he really does love me?* Everyone doesn't know how to show love properly, especially someone who grew without the love of a father.

Unlike a lot of people, I grew up with both my parents who were still married. While they had disagreements like any other couple, they were never disrespectful to each other, and the love they shared was visible. They had an old-school kind of love that is rarely seen but often longed for, one built from a genuine appreciation for each other.

The kind I wanted.

There were no surprise children popping up out of the woodwork, and my father put his family first at all times. I couldn't think of a time I'd seen my mother crying on account of my father, unless they were happy tears. And yet, I'd ended up with a man who had made me cry on more occasions than I could count. With all of the positive examples of real love that I got from my parents, it was shocking that I'd ended up married to a man I barely knew. The fact that I was married to a man who had lied to me since the beginning of our relationship, who tricked me into marrying him and who was a convicted felon in county lock up, was a hard pill to swallow. While I was disappointed in everything that Kyle had put me through, I was more disappointed in myself.

"I think I just need some time to figure out how to move forward. I can't lie and act like I don't love you, Kyle. I wouldn't have married you if I didn't. But you have to admit, in the short time we've been together, we've been through a lot. More than a normal couple. So much that I'm too embarrassed to talk to anyone about it. Since all of this went down, I have been avoiding my parents, I've been avoiding Toni. I'm tired of putting up a front like everything is perfect."

"I understand, Nakia..."

"You have one-minute remaining for this call," an electronic voice said interrupting our conversation.

"Look, baby," he said hurriedly. "I just want you to know that I love you, and I will spend the rest of my life making this up to you if you let me. Just hold me down, and I promise I'm going to give you the world. I'll talk to you soon, okay?"

"Okay."

The call disconnected before we could say goodbye. I can't say I felt any better than I had before the phone call. I was still uncertain how to move forward with our relationship, and while I felt Kyle meant it when he'd said he loved me, I wasn't sure if the love he had to offer was enough. I needed more.

CHAPTER 13

ONE YEAR LATER

"Girl, thank goodness I caught a train instead of driving, 'cuz I'm starting to feel twisted," Toni said, dramatically fanning herself.

While I worked on my lobster bisque, Toni had just finished what had to be her fifth drink in less than an hour, and I could tell she was more than tipsy.

"Girl, you better slow down. Nobody wants your drunk behind on their train," I said teased.

Toni was in town for business, and we had arranged to hang out for a while before she headed back to Virginia. A year had passed since Kyle had gone to jail, and I wanted to tell Toni everything that had happened between us. She knew he'd been locked up, but I hadn't told her about the pregnancy and the miscarriage. It sucked not being able to just talk openly and share my feelings with her, but my pride wouldn't let me. Not that Toni would have judged me or anything, it was really all in my head. I was judging myself, and that was enough to keep me quiet.

"So, how's Kyle doing?" Toni asked with a slight hint of sass. "He only has about eight more months left, right?"

"Only? Girl, eight months is a long time. Believe me, you'd never want to go through something like this."

"I bet. But I know you been getting you a little something on the side while he's been locked up, right? I couldn't imagine going all that time without sex."

"Nope," I replied before taking a sip of my cocktail. "I haven't been with anyone else." Toni stared at me with wide eyes from across the table.

"Nobody? Are you serious?"

"Yes, Toni. I take my vows seriously."

Truthfully, it was hard not being with a man, but I managed. Of course, there were times when I yearned for a man's touch, but I didn't want to add any more negative energy into the mix of our relationship by cheating on him. After Kyle and I spoke about the miscarriage, I'd decided that despite everything, I wanted our relationship to work, otherwise everything would have been for nothing. Besides, I've never been a quitter.

I caught up with Toni until the restaurant closed, then offered to drive her to the train station, even though it was a little out of my way. Toni was very drunk, and I wanted to make sure she made it.

After dropping her off, I was about to head home when my gas light came on. It was late, and I really didn't want to stop due to the area I was in, but I also didn't want to get stuck on the side of the road, so I pulled into a Shell station in South East.

Determined to make it fast, I walked into the mini-mart to pay for the gas before returning promptly to the pump.

Just as I was finishing up, a shiny black *Infiniti* pulled up to the pump next to me. The windows were tinted, and I could feel the bassline vibrating from the rap music, blasting through the speakers. *Drug dealer*, I immediately thought. But, as I got ready to enter my car, I couldn't help but notice the fine specimen of a man who stepped out.

The first things I noticed were his fresh *Timbs*, and how confident he stood in them. He sported stylish designer jeans, a fresh white T, and a lightweight leather jacket. He was tall and had a muscular build that let me know he went to the gym often. My eyes devoured the rest of him in seconds. He had a caramel completion with reddish undertones and appeared to be Dominican. His face was beautiful. He had high defined cheekbones, dark brown piercing eyes accentuated by his dark thick eyebrows, and jet-black hair that was low cut with waves.

Before I could turn away from staring to hard, he caught my gaze and smiled. My heart raced with excitement as I gave him a slight smile back. To my surprise, he began to walk toward me. Remembering what neighborhood, I was in, I hoped he wasn't trying to rob me. Then I remembered what he was driving and realized I had nothing worthy for him to rob.

I kept my guard up and let his smile capture my full attention, rather than jumping into my car and driving off. I was curious to find out what he wanted.

"Hi, my name is David," he said flashing that same sexy smile that caught my attention in the first place. "You're not from around here, are you?"

Damn, is it that obvious? I wondered. "No, not really. I was just driving home and had to get gas."

"I see. What's your name?"

"Nakia." I said trying to tame the Cheshire cat smile I had on my face. David was fine as hell, and as he stood in front of me, I couldn't help but imagine his strong, muscular body intertwined with mine. After all, it had been over a year since the last time I'd had any. I felt like I would burst just at the sound of his sultry voice.

"If you're not from around here, why are you here so late and all alone?"

"I just dropped a friend off at the train station. I'm headed home now."

"Do you mind if I ask where home is?"

"Maybe I do mind. You sure do ask a lot of question for someone I don't know."

"Oh, my bad. I thought we were getting to know each other?" he replied, smiling.

That damn smile, and those mesmerizing eyes were trying

to get me in trouble. "Oh, is that what we're doing?" I asked, smiling back. *Now, I know this negro sees my wedding ring.*

"That's what I'm trying to do. But look, it's late, and I don't want to keep you out if you were heading home. How about you give me your number, and I can call you. Maybe we can hang out sometime."

Although I knew it was dead wrong for me to give my number to another man while I was a married woman, it felt good to capture a man's attention for a change. What could I say? David had an aura about him that intrigued me and excited me in ways I hadn't been in quite a while. I needed to find out what this sexy stranger with the fly car was about. But the bottom line was I was tired of being lonely.

After writing down my number on the gas station receipt, and handing it to him, we said goodbye, and I got into my car to drive home. As I drove, I was all smiles. *Would he really call?* I was so excited by the possibilities that I almost forgot I was married.

The excitement quickly turned to guilt, however, when I got home and found a letter from Kyle in the mailbox. *Damn. What was I thinking?*

After reading Kyle's letter, I felt even guiltier. Kyle had made a lot of mistakes over the course of our relationship, but I knew he truly loved me, and I couldn't deny the fact that I loved him too. While having an attractive man approach me and ask to get to know me was flattering, I knew I'd have to let David know about my situation when he called—if he called. That man could've been full of it, and as far as I was concerned, there was no way he didn't notice my wedding band.

A few days passed and I'd pretty much determined David had no intentions of calling me. While I was kind of relieved, I was also a bit disappointed. *Why ask for someone's number if you don't plan on calling them?*

Friday night rolled around and with no class or work to occupy my time, I was bored out of my mind. I decided to uncork a bottle of wine and review my DVD collection. I landed on season four of *The Wire*, my favorite season. I downed my first glass of wine quickly and immediately poured another. Before I knew it, the bottle was half a glass shy of being empty. I was buzzed and hadn't even made it through the first episode of the show. *What a wino*, I thought to myself.

My phone rang, and I had every intention on ignoring it, but I figured I could use some conversation, after all who wants to be tipsy and silent. By the fourth ring I answered, not bothering to look at the caller ID.

"Nakia?" A sultry voice asked.

To my surprise it was David. Maybe it was the wine, maybe I was just lonely and feeling reckless, but everything that happened next was totally beyond my normal behavior. From the moment I heard his voice, I knew I wanted to see him. Less than five minutes into our conversation, I invited him over.

Dimly, I felt some sense of regret when we hung up the phone. I knew inviting him over was a huge mistake. I knew nothing good could come of it, but it was too late. He was already on his way.

Realizing I was in no way prepared for company, I took a quick shower, slipped into some shorts and a tank top, put my hair up in a top knot and applied some light makeup. Then, I ran around like a mad woman attempting to tidy up. I shook my head as I glanced inside refrigerator. All I could offer was water and wine, so I made a mental note to go grocery shopping the next morning. Since Kyle had been away, I'd mainly been eating take out. I had just finishing straightening up my apartment when I heard a knock on my door.

I took a quick look at myself in my hall mirror before opening the door.

As soon as I laid eyes on him, all panic and worry escaped me. He looked better than I'd remembered. We exchanged approving glances, after we'd both taken a moment to look each other up and down.

"Hey," I said before ushering him into my apartment. "Come on in." His cologne was mesmerizing, and his wardrobe was just as clean as the night I'd met him.

"Would you like something to drink?" I asked after he was seated.

"Nah, I'm good, shorty. Come sit down next to me." He patted the space on the sofa next to him.

"Oh, okay. One minute. I need a drink."

My heart was racing a mile a minute. *What was I getting myself into?* After pouring another glass of wine for myself, I took a sip before sitting down beside him. His scent was more intoxicating than the wine.

"You know, I'm kind of surprised you invited me over. Especially since it appears you have a man and all." He nodded to one of the pictures on the wall, the one Kyle and I had taken right after we'd gotten married. "What's up with that?"

A sense of sadness came over me. There I was, sitting on the couch next to a man I was obviously attracted to, while a picture of my husband and I hung on the wall across from us. *What was wrong with me?* "Yeah, I'm married. But...it's complicated."

"Oh, damn. So, am I gonna have to worry about a crazy dude running up on me?" he asked, with a concerned look.

"Nope. He's locked up," I replied bluntly. "I'm sorry. I probably shouldn't have invited you over," I said softly.

There was a brief silence before he spoke. "Nah, it's cool. Let me guess, you're lonely?"

I nodded. "Yeah. I'm really not the type of woman to invite random men into my home, I promise you. I just felt like I needed some male company. When you approached me at the gas station that night, it just felt good to be noticed by someone new. I'm sorry if I mislead you."

"Don't worry about it. You're good. I'm glad you invited me over," he replied reassuringly.

The way he looked me in the eyes as he spoke made me feel

so secure. It was like he'd never lie to me—unlike my trifling ass husband.

"I had a feeling you weren't *that* type of woman anyway. I'm cool just chilling and talking. If that's okay with you?"

I grinned. "No, I'm really not. And thank you. I could really use someone to talk to these days."

The rest of the evening was spent getting to know each other. I learned that he grew up with a single mother, that he was Dominican, born and raised in Baltimore, and that he was currently living in D.C. He was twenty-six years old and he confirmed he was *not* a drug dealer like I had previously wondered, but rather he was an event promoter, well known on the club scene in the DMV area. He had no kids and he was single. I found the single part hard to believe because he was so damn attractive. But he insisted he was, so I took his word for it.

As if her were my therapist, I divulged everything about me, including everything that had taken place between Kyle and I. The wine was definitely making me more comfortable than usual, because I had not shared that information with anyone else. He was very attentive as he listened to me and it seemed like he was truly interested in what I was saying. He didn't criticize me for my choices, and before I knew it, we had stayed up talking until almost daybreak.

At some point, the wine I'd been sipping on must have taken its toll because I fell asleep. All I remembered was being woken up as David carried me to my bed, followed by a gentle kiss on my forehead. I fell back to sleep immediately afterward.

David was a gentleman the entire time, and while our attraction for one another was obvious, he made sure not to go too far out of respect for my marriage. I appreciated that, because Lord knew, had he tried something I wouldn't have stopped him.

When I woke up the next morning, David was gone, but there was a little note on my nightstand that read:

I'm looking forward to our friendship. I'll call you later. - D.

I smiled from ear to ear the rest of the day.

CHAPTER 14

Over the next three months, my friendship with David grew. We spent a lot of our time together when we weren't working, and he was always respectful. We did flirt at times, but it never went beyond words. But I couldn't pretend like David wasn't having an impact on me emotionally. The more time we spent together, the less I visited Kyle. I started to not answer his calls or return his letters as often until I barely did at all. While a part of me wanted to work on my marriage, another part of me wanted to explore the possibilities with David. We even had nicknames for each other. He called me "angel face" because he said I looked like an angel when I slept, and I called him "handsome face" because there was no better way to describe how fine he was.

One night, as I was getting dressed for an event David was taking me to, my phone rang. I didn't recognize the number, but

I answered anyway. As soon as I heard the voice on the other end, my heart sank. It was Kyle. He'd somehow arranged for one of his family members to call me on three-way and needless to say he was pissed.

"Where the hell have you been, Nakia? Why have you been avoiding my calls and not coming to visit? I haven't seen you or my son! I have to get my family to call you just to get you to pick up the phone. What the hell is going on?"

I took a deep breath. I didn't know how to respond, and I knew the time would come when I'd have to give Kyle some answers. But now wasn't the time. Sure, I felt bad for not bringing Kyle Jr. to see him; Tamika didn't have a car, so she couldn't bring him herself. I'd been ignoring her calls too, but all the craziness Kyle had put me through made me feel justified in my actions. After all it was his fault, he was in the situation he was in.

So, I said what I'd contemplated saying to him since almost the beginning of our marriage. "I want a divorce."

"What? Are you serious? Look, baby, we're almost at the end of this. I'm not even mad at you for not coming up here or answering my calls. I can only imagine how hard it's been for you and when I told you I'd make it up to you for the rest of my life, I meant it. I've just been worried about you. I'm sorry for yelling. Please, just think this through."

"That's the thing, Kyle, I have thought about it. To be honest, that's all I've done is think about it, and the more I think about it, the more I know we're not going to make it through this. I wish I felt differently, but I don't. We've grown apart."

His next question came out quick, as if it had been the only thing on his mind. "Is there someone else?"

I let the silence grow while I thought about how to answer him. I hadn't cheated on him; David and I had kept things entirely platonic. But I had feelings for him. I didn't want to lie to Kyle, but the answer was complicated.

"Nakia, are you fucking someone else?"

I wanted to lie to him and tell him yes, but I could hear the pain in his voice. I wanted him to hurt like he'd hurt me. I wanted him to feel pain like I'd felt since he'd been gone, but I couldn't lie to him. He's lied enough for the both of us.

"No, Kyle. I'm not fucking someone else."

As if on cue, I heard a knock on my apartment door, and knew it was David.

"Look, I gotta go. I can't do this right now," I said, before hanging up the phone.

After taking a deep breath, I got myself together, before opening the door for David. "Hey, handsome face."

Despite things being left in limbo with Kyle, I continued to spend time with David. I told him about the phone conversation and how I'd told him I wanted a divorce, hoping that it would help us to get to the next level in whatever we had going on. David assured me he was feeling me as much as I was feeling him. He also told me he was hesitant about taking things to the next level until the divorce was final. I respected his feelings and we continued on as usual.

Surprisingly, I didn't receive any further phone calls or letters from Kyle, and while I wanted to act like I was finally free of him, I knew I'd have to deal with our situation at some point. I just didn't know how soon.

It was sixteen months into Kyle's sentence, and I had just arrived at my apartment from work. I was tired, but I had plans to go to dinner with David, so I'd left work a little early so that I'd have time to get dressed.

As I turned the corner of the hallway of my apartment building, I stopped dead in my tracks. There was Kyle, leaning against my apartment door, looking straight at me. He was much more muscular than the last time I'd see him, and his expression wasn't the same as the one I was used to.

"Hey, Nakia."

"Kyle," I was in shock. I couldn't believe he was there in front of me. He wasn't supposed to get released for another couple of months. "How are you here?"

"Damn, I would've thought you would be happier to see me. No hug, no kiss, just 'how are you here?'

"I'm sorry, I just didn't expect to see you. I didn't expect you to be released this, soon," I said as I opened to door and we entered the apartment.

I didn't know how to feel about Kyle being there. I also

knew I'd need to let David know what was up before I had a major problem on my hands.

After we came inside, I glanced around to make sure there were no remnants of David laying around. While David and I weren't sleeping together, we did spend a lot of time together, and it was possible he'd left an item or two in my apartment. I was silent as I watched Kyle walk around the apartment, like he was inspecting it, as if he expected to find signs of another man as well.

Finally, he walked into the living room and sat on the sofa.

"They let me out early on good behavior. I would've called you, but based on our last conversation, I figured I'd give you time to think."

All I could think about was calling David to let him know Kyle was back. I really didn't need a fight breaking out in my apartment, and I had no clue how Kyle would react if another man showed up at my door.

Unexpectedly, my phone rang. I walked over to the cordless phone and glanced at the caller ID. *Shit.* It was David.

"Hey, what's up?" I said cheerily into the phone. I wanted Kyle to think it was one of my girlfriends.

"Hey, angel face. Nothing much, I'm just calling to let you know I'm running a little late, but I'll be there within the hour."

"Actually, I'm sitting here talking with Kyle. He's home early, so we have a lot to catch up on. But I'll talk to you later, okay?"

"Wait, what? Kyle? As in your husband?" The disappointment in his voice was obvious.

"Yeah, so I'm gonna call you later, okay?" Then, before he could say another word, I hung up the phone.

"Who was that?" Kyle asked.

"Oh, that was Toni. She didn't want anything. I told her I'll call her later." It seemed as if he believed me.

"So, what's up with us Nakia? You still on that divorce bullshit?"

I plopped down on the chair across from him, defeated. As I took off my heels and arched my feet, I could see him looking me up and down.

"Come here," he said, motioning for me to sit next to him.

I was slightly uncomfortable and nervous, but I walked over to sit next to him, and he maneuvered me so that my legs were stretched across his lap. Then he took my foot in his hand and began to massage it so intensely that my body instantly relaxed.

After he'd massaged both of my feet, his hands moved up to my calves, and then under my dress and up my legs to my inner thighs. I could feel myself getting moist as his fingers grazed across my panties, and my legs began to tremble from his touch. I missed being touched. I needed to feel him. I hadn't been with anyone in that way since before he'd gone to jail.

Suddenly, Kyle raised my hips up to remove my panties, then placed my legs on his shoulders. I was in bliss as I felt his tongue trace across my inner thighs, then between my legs, sucking gently on my pearl.

What started off as soft and gentle gradually progressed into passion as he sucked and licked until I was ready to orgasm. Then, just as I was about to climax, he stood up and removed his sweatpants and boxers, before thrusting his hardness into my warm core. Each pulse made me feel as though I was going to explode. Tears streamed down my face as my fingernails dug into his back, each stroke bringing me closer and closer to ecstasy.

As he kissed on my neck, breasts, and lips, I slowly began to remember everything I loved about him. As I moaned his name during my climax, David began to fade further and further from my thoughts.

We made love passionately for hours until we were both spent, and as we lay together in each other's embrace when we were done, I knew I couldn't let my husband go. The grip he had on me was too strong, and even David couldn't break his hold. At that moment, I knew I'd give Kyle another chance. I just didn't know what I was going to do about David.

CHAPTER 15

Kyle had been home for a few months, and we picked up with married life as if he'd never been gone. He was able to get his old job back at one of the local clubs, and we were even trying to get pregnant again. Our bond with Kyle Jr. was getting better and he stayed with us quite often. I'd even made it a point to visit my parents more, so they could get to know Kyle. Things seemed to be going well. Kyle was thinking about returning to school to get his master's, and I was one semester away from finishing my law degree.

Things were getting back on track.

I came home one day to find Kyle sitting on the couch. His eyes were red and puffy like he'd been crying.

"Babe, what's wrong?" I asked.

I'd expected him to be getting ready for his job at the club, but I could tell from his expression something was seriously wrong. He buried his head in his hands as I sat down next to him, but he didn't say anything. All I could do was rub his back gently and wait.

When he was finally ready, he looked up at me.

"My cousin Kevin was shot and killed a few hours ago. My mother called to give me the news."

I didn't know Kevin very well, but I'd met him a few times since I'd been with Kyle. The two of them had grown up together and were more like brothers than cousins. I knew my husband was hurting. While Kyle didn't talk much about his upbringing, I knew that he grew up in the hood and, while Kyle had chosen the college route, Kevin had chosen the streets. It was sad, but that unfortunately was the fate of many young black men nowadays.

Kyle was quiet over the next couple of days. He'd called out of work and wasn't doing much but drinking and smoking weed. While I hated the constant smell in my apartment, I let it go because I knew he was grieving. I just hoped he'd get over it soon because I refused to watch all the progress he'd made go down the drain.

Kevin's funeral was the Saturday after he died, and even though I hated funerals and considered staying home, I went because I knew Kyle needed my support.

As we walked into the church, I hugged and greeted some of the family members I knew, before sitting towards the back of the church, while Kyle walked to the front to sit with the family and other pallbearers.

As I watched Kyle walk to the front and take a seat, my heart stopped as David's familiar face caught my eye.

What is he doing here? I couldn't believe it. Only in my world would the dude I was falling for while my husband was in jail, somehow know my husband's family. I just hoped by some miracle David wouldn't notice me.

Everything was fine until the end of the service when David, who was also a pallbearer, walked past my pew. He glanced in my direction, and we caught each other's gaze. From the look on his face, I could tell he was just as shocked as I was to see him there. He noticed Kyle looking at me, and he was putting two-and-two together.

Shit. Please don't let this end up in disaster.

During the repass, I tried to keep cool and stay to myself. Kyle came by to check on me every once in a while, but he was completely drunk, so I let him hang out with his family. I hadn't seen David since we'd arrived at the repass and I was hoping he'd chosen not to come.

But, no such luck. An hour in, I spotted David, and he was headed in my direction. I quickly looked around to see where Kyle was. He was busy in another part of the room talking with family. I took a deep breath as David sat down at the table next to me.

"What's up, Nakia?" he asked.

I could sense he was a little angry with me since I'd pretty much ghosted him, but what did he expect? Kyle was my husband. I just hoped he wouldn't make a scene.

"Hey, David. Small world, I see?"

"Yeah, it really is," he said, shaking his head.

It was silent between us for a moment.

"So, I guess you decided to give ol' boy another chance?" he said, nodding in Kyle's direction.

"Yeah, I did," I said sort of absentmindedly, something was bothering me. "Do you know Kyle?"

"Nah, I don't know him. I met Kevin a few years ago when I was staying in Virginia with my cousin Mark. He's the tall guy over in the corner," he said, pointing in the direction where Kyle was. "We've been cool ever since. I know his mother and everything, but surprisingly, I've never met Kyle."

"I see," I replied.

I caught a glimpse of Kyle drunkenly stumbling toward us. As he got closer, I got more and more nervous, wondering if he suspected anything.

"What's good, my man?"

"Nothing much. What's good with you?" David replied.

My heart was racing. Their acidic tones let me know they weren't being cordial.

"I don't know. I'm just wondering why, out of all the seats in this room, you're over here with my wife? I know you see that ring on her finger."

I'd never seen Kyle act jealous over me, and I had a feeling the alcohol was the blame.

David smiled. "Chill. We're just talking. It's nothing serious, I was just leaving. You take care, Nakia. Okay?"

"Wait, you told this motherfucker your name? You know this dude?"

Before I could respond, David stood up facing Kyle. David had a good three inches in height on Kyle, but Kyle was definitely the more muscular of the two.

"Calm, down. It's not that serious. You don't need to speak to her that way."

"Man, get the fuck outta my face. That's my wife!" Kyle said, before pushing David away.

Wrong move. Before I knew it, both Kyle and David were throwing punches in the middle of the repass. Frozen in my seat, I watched helplessly. *This would happen to me.*

A few of Kyle's cousins rushed over to break up the fight. I was too through at this point though. *Who fights at a freaking repass?*

After things had calmed down, and David had left, I stood up and headed to the exit myself. Kyle had been out of order, and I didn't care if he was leaving with me or not. All I knew was judging from all the side-eyes Kyle's family was giving me, it was time for me to go.

I was about halfway to my car when I heard footsteps running up behind me.

"Kia, wait up," Kyle huffed.

I turned around to face him. He looked disheveled and several buttons were missing from his dress shirt. "What do you want?"

"Look, I'm sorry. I didn't mean to act that way. I'm tripping because of my cousin, that's all. I shouldn't have put my hands on that man."

"No shit, Kyle. You've been acting real different lately. I know your cousin just died, so I was letting all the drinking and smoking you've been doing lately be, but this was too much. What were you thinking?" He could press charges! You could wind up back in jail if he pressed charges!"

Kyle hung his head in shame. "I know. I'm sorry." He stood there quietly for a few moments.

"Well, I think it's best that I head home."

"I think I'm going to kick it with my family for a little while longer. I'll get a ride back to D.C. with my boy."

"Okay, I'll talk to you later," I said, before turning to walk toward my car and driving home.

I waited up past midnight for Kyle, but he never came home that night and I was reminded of the loneliness and deceit I'd felt during the first year of our marriage.

CHAPTER 16

FIVE MONTHS LATER

Kyle had changed since the funeral and that caused changes between us. He was still working, but he wasn't putting much energy into our relationship, and he was spending almost every weekend he didn't work in Richmond at his dad's. While at first, he claimed he was going back and forth to spend time with his son, I could tell after a while that he just didn't want to be around me. I didn't know what I'd done to him to make him act that way, but it was getting to the point where I didn't care either. I'd set up a face-to-face meeting with the same attorney's office I had contacted a while back. It was crazy because as I thought about everything that had happened, I couldn't help but think that I'd missed out on a good thing by choosing Kyle over a potentially better man.

It was a Thursday night, and Kyle was working at the club.

I was cooking dinner for myself when the phone rang. I picked it up and was surprised by the voice on the other end.

"Hey, Nakia. How have you been?"

"Jerell?" I said, surprised. I was flooded with emotion but held it in to avoid sounding desperate. "Hey, I'm good. How are you?"

It had seemed like forever since I'd heard his voice. I hadn't realized how much I'd missed him these past few years.

"How am I doing? Well, it depends on your answer to my next question. Are you still married?" I could tell by his voice that he was teasing.

"Yes, Jerell. I'm still married," I replied with an empty chuckle. "But, how have you been? How is the modeling going?"

"Everything is good on my end. I just got back from Europe a few weeks ago. You've actually been on my mind for a few weeks now, so, I figured I'd take a risk and call you, hoping your man wouldn't answer."

"Nah, he's at work right now."

As Jerell and I caught each other up on our respective lives, I couldn't help but think how different my life would've been had I stayed with him. I had a feeling that if I would have given Jerell more time, I would've been a lot happier than I was in my current relationship. Jerell had heard all about Kyle's sentencing, and when I asked him why he'd never called me, he told me he was still kind of angry with me for how things ended. After I told him about the miscarriage, he apologized for not checking in on me sooner.

Two hours later, we started to wrap up our conversation.

"I mean it, Nakia. You are a beautiful and intelligent woman, and you've got your whole life ahead of you. It's not too late to find true love. I just want you to be happy."

The sincerity in his voice gave me hope and a willingness to find true love in the future. I didn't know if Jerell was right for me, but my Mr. Right was out there, somewhere. "Thanks, Jerell."

After hanging up with him, I thought about all that we'd talked about. It was as if everyone else could see the truth about Kyle except me. I was twenty-six years old and had been married to Kyle since the ripe young age of twenty-three, with about seventy-five percent of our marriage spent apart. Throughout most of our marriage, I'd literally been a single wife. I'd gone back and forth about divorcing him several times, but I knew that I had to be serious and let him know it wasn't working. I refused to let good sex change my mind.

A few nights later, Kyle and I were lying in bed, and I was trying to think of a way to tell him that I wanted a divorce. As he cuddled up behind me, I could tell he wanted some, but I refused to fall for it. I was only nine on Sunday evening, but I pretended like I was asleep, hoping he'd get the hint. After a while, he gave up, and I eventually did fall asleep.

I awoke a few hours later to a pitch-black room and an empty bed. I got up to use the bathroom. I walked through the living room to the kitchen. No Kyle. I decided to grab a bottle of water from the fridge when I noticed my keys were missing. Kyle was off work that night, so I wondered where he had gone. His car had recently broken down, so we were sharing until he could save up enough to buy a new one.

Figuring he had run to the store or something, I sat down in the living room to wait for him. An hour went by before I picked up the phone to call his cell. It went straight to voice-mail. I must have called him fifty more times that night to no avail. *Where was this negro at with my car, knowing I needed to go to work in the morning?*

Sometime around five that morning I called into work and left a message telling my boss that I wouldn't be in. It was a Monday morning, and I hated calling off on Mondays, but what choice did I have? I'd given up on calling Kyle and the longer I waited, the angrier I became.

This man must have lost his goddamn mind! It wasn't until a quarter to five Monday evening when I finally heard back from him.

"Where the hell are you, Kyle?"

"Nakia, I'm sorry. I had to handle some things, and unfortunately, I got pulled over."

"What?" I asked but shrugged off my concern and confusion. I didn't have the emotional capacity to really care anymore. "Where is my car?"

"Your car is fine. I'm about to drive home right now. Baby, I'm so sorry. None of this was supposed to happen."

"What are you even doing? Why'd you leave? Why did you get pulled over?"

"I—I was speeding. I was trying to get back home before you had to go to work. I left last night while you were asleep. It was supposed to be a quick run down here and back, but with my luck, of course I got pulled over."

"Down where? Where the hell are you Kyle?"

There was a pause before he spoke. "North Carolina."

"Are you fucking serious? North Carolina, Kyle? What the hell is in North Carolina and why'd you have to leave in the middle of the night in secrecy? Not only are you putting my job in jeopardy, but you didn't think it was important for you to ask me before you took my car out of state?"

"I'm sorry, Nakia. I needed the money. You know I have to pay five hundred dollar every month, and working security isn't cutting it. So, when my cousin Tyrone hit me up and asked me to make a run for him, I agreed. He's helped me out in the past, so I owed him. Shit never works out the way I plan, but I'm trying. I'm trying my best, Kia. I'm sorry. I'm sorry for all of this."

My blood was boiling. "Yeah, you really are sorry. You've been sorry this entire relationship. But you know what? I'm glad this happened. You just confirmed my decision to finally divorce your sorry ass. I can't wait for the meeting I have scheduled with my attorney. You're a selfish liar. You don't care about me. You care about what you gain from being with me. And now you have the nerve to run some drug shit in my car? I don't need this, Kyle. Bring me my car. I think you need to call your father —or hell, even Tyrone to help you collect your shit. It's over. I am not doing this anymore!"

Before I had a chance to change my mind, I hung up.

Even though I was pissed, I felt freer than I'd felt in a long time. I was finally about to get my life back. I was finally leaving Kyle and he knew it. So many emotions were going through me that I broke down and cried. But they weren't tears of sadness, they were tears of release. It was truly time for me to move on.

Kyle arrived shortly after ten that night. To my surprise, he didn't even try to ask for my forgiveness. Something about the way I looked at him when he walked through the door must've told him I was serious. As I lay in my bed, I watched him walk back and forth between the bedroom and the living room as he packed his things. I was so sick of him that I was counting down the hours until he was gone for good. I had already taken off the next day for my appointment with the lawyer. It was finally time to end this marriage, and as the hours wound down, I was becoming more excited by the moment.

Kyle's father arrived early the next morning and helped him put his things in the car. Once they were done, Kyle placed his keys on the counter and left.

That was it. No long, drawn-out goodbyes. No begging me to reconsider. He simply left, and I knew it was better that way.

As I took in my apartment, I felt a sense of freedom that I hadn't felt in a long time. I would miss Kyle, but in my heart, I knew it was time for our relationship to end. Maybe it was the fact that we're were born only a week apart and that we're both Geminis, because our connection was surreal. It's as if we were twin flames the way I felt on fire every time he made love to me. But sexual energy only lasts so long, and it was time I put that fire out. It was finally over.

CHAPTER 17

SIX MONTHS LATER

Since Kyle and I had broken up, though I'd given in a few times and let him get some, I never let him move back in, and I never agreed to get back together with him. I only called him over when I wanted sex, that was the least he could do. The fire between us was gone though, and I eventually ended the booty calls too. Instead, I started working on self-care and getting my mind right. After living in the same apartment since my internship, I knew it was time for a change. My salary had grown significantly since I'd moved in, and I'd decided it was time to upgrade. I'd also gotten the divorce papers from my lawyer, and all I needed was Kyle's signature to make everything final.

Life was great. I'd finally completed my law degree and was working as a contract attorney for the government. I had become friends with some of my colleagues and we went out together regularly. I even went on a vacation to Paris with Toni for two weeks. Everything was looking up, and I knew ending things with Kyle was one of the best things I'd ever done. The only thing I regretted was not leaving him sooner.

After searching for the right place for months, I'd finally settled on a beautiful townhouse in Bowie, Maryland, not far from where I worked in D.C. I had just finished putting the last box of clothing into my trunk, when I saw Kyle driving up in his father's car. For some reason I was nervous. The last couple of times I'd seen him, we were in bed together, but I kept my poker face on and reminded myself it was strictly business as he approached me in the parking lot.

"Hey Kyle, you remember Cleo, right? She is going to notarize the documents for us."

"Hey. Good seeing you again, Cleo" he replied.

"Same here, Kyle," Cleo replied.

"So, this is it, huh?" he immediately turned toward me and grabbed the divorce papers lying on the hood of my car. He idly flipped through them.

"Yeah," I said softly before handing him a pen.

A sense of peace came over me as I watched him sign the papers. As he handed the papers back to me, I could see the sadness in his eyes. I felt bad for him. I signed the papers before handing them to Cleo. Finally, that crazy chapter of my life was coming to a close. While I was no longer in love with him, I wasn't sure about his feelings for me had subsided.

"All right, you two are all set. Best of luck to you both. Keep

in touch Nakia," Cleo stated before handing me the now nota-
rized paperwork.

"Thanks, Cleo," Kyle and I said in unison as she walked off.

"I'm sorry things ended up this way, Nakia. You are the
best thing that has happened to me, and even if it was only for a
moment, I'm thankful for the time we shared. I really wish you
the best."

"Thank you, I wish you the best too."

We gave each other a quick hug before he got into his car
and drove off. As I watched him disappear down the street, I
inhaled deeply. I felt on top of the world. I was excited about
everything that was yet to come and most importantly, I was
thankful for closure. While things hadn't ended as planned
with Kyle, I remained faithful that I would eventually find my
Mr. Right. But, until then, I was determined to live my best life
and be patient. I would no longer rush into relationships. If I
met someone new, fine, but I wasn't pressed. I was determined
to live freely and completely first and foremost. Most of all, I
would set standards for myself, and implement them for any
man I decided to let into my life. I would do my best to avoid
decepticons and I'd make sure I'd test every man I met for
lieabetes, because there was no way in hell I would allow
myself to become anyone's single wife again. That chapter of
my life was closed for good, and I was never looking back. I
would take time to repair my heart and love on myself before
loving someone else.

And, most importantly, I would live.

AFTERWORD

It was a hot spring day, and I was packing a bag to head to Ocean City with a few friends. I had spent a lot of time with myself in the past few months and it was nice to finally have some social interaction. I had come to terms with the fact that I lost some of my self-worth after Kyle and by dating and relearning myself, I was able regain the confidence I had lost. It felt good to reclaim my sanity and it helped me wash away the deceit I'd endured. I came to the realization that I was impatient and searching for something that I had no control over. In my relationships, I failed to consider that, if meant to be, things would happen the right way and at the right time. With all of that behind me self-love was my focus and it felt good.

I finished packing my bag and loaded up the car. I ran back inside to grab a bottle of water when my house phone rang. After looking at the caller ID, I grabbed it on the third ring.

"Hey, mom. Why don't you ever call my cell phone? I'm about to get rid of this house phone soon. I's using my cell phone for all calls now and no one really has a house phone anymore anyway."

"Girl, you better not get rid of your house phone. What would happen if those things suddenly stopped working? I don't trust all of that new technology."

"Ma, you don't trust anything made after 1970. But, I'm on my way out the door I'm heading to the beach with a few friends. Did you need something?"

"Well, I was calling you to tell you I ran into that boy you used to date. What's his name? Jarrett, Gerald?"

"Jerell, mom?"

"Yes, Jerell. That's his name. I ran into him at the mall, and he was looking as handsome as ever. I'll never understand why you broke up with that boy for that Kyle."

"Well, that was a long time ago, mama. What's done is done."

"Well, it doesn't have to be. I talked to him for a good while, and I don't think he's gotten over you. Plus, he's single, and I don't think he lives too far from you. You better give him a call."

I smiled at my mom's attempts to play matchmaker. "Mom, I haven't spoken with Jerell in months. We're two different people now. Besides, I don't even think I have his number anymore."

"That's okay. He'll probably be calling you because I gave him your new number and address. You can thank me later."

"Mom," I groaned. "Why?" My mother had good intentions, but I didn't want her involved in my love life. After all I just wanted to focus on me. "Never mind. I have to go now, but I'll call you when I get back. Tell dad I said hi, okay?"

"Okay, baby. Love you."

"I love you too, mom," I replied, before hanging up. Then I picked up my bag and headed out the door.

I had just closed the trunk when I heard a familiar voice behind me. I turned around only to see one of the finest men I'd ever seen in my life.

"Nakia?" he asked, shaking his head. "Damn, it's a small world."

All I could do was smile. Things were about to get interesting.

THANK YOU

Thank you for reading *The Single Wife*. If you enjoyed it, please take a moment to leave a review on Amazon, Barnes and Noble, Goodreads, or your preferred online retailer.

Reviews are the best way to show your support for an author and to help new readers discover their books.

ABOUT THE AUTHOR

Marquita B. is currently working in Product Development for an Insurance Company. She is also the proud founder of Corks and Coils Publishing.

Born in Nyack, NY and in her teenage years raised in Lynchburg, VA, Marquita B. has an entrepreneurial spirit with a passion for writing. After obtaining her master's she moved to the DC area, where she enjoys spending time with her husband and daughter. Her spare time is spent watching reality TV or HGTV, singing, cooking, searching for hair care products, wine tasting and shopping.

"The Single Wife" is her debut novella and is the first in the "Journeys of the Heart" trilogy.